Copyright © 2023 by Sammi Mason.

All rights reserved.

No part of this publication may be reproduced, distributed, or transmitted in any form or by any means, including photocopying, recording, or other electronic or mechanical methods, without the prior written permission of the publisher, except as permitted by U.S. copyright law. For permission requests, contact sammi@sammimasonauthor.com.

The story, all names, characters, and incidents portrayed in this production are fictitious. No identification with actual persons (living or deceased), places, buildings, and products is intended or should be inferred.

Book Cover by GetCovers

One edition 2023

Contents

Title Page	V
1. One	1
2. Two	16
3. Three	33
4. Four	43
5. Five	60
6. Six	70
7. Seven	84
8. Eight	93
9. Nine	104
10. Ten	116
11. Eleven	128
12. Twelve	140
13. Thirteen	154

14.	Fourteen	164
15.	Fifteen	177
16.	Sixteen	194
17.	Seventeen	203
18.	Eighteen	212
19.	Nineteen	221
20.	Twenty	233
21.	Twenty-One	250
22.	Twenty-Two	257
A Note From Sammi		269

A Genie's New Start

A Paranormal Women's Fiction Novel

Sammi Mason

One

I catch a final desolate glimpse of the house that has been my home for the last decade. The cozy family life I lived within its dark brick walls plays through my exhausted mind, further shattering my grieving heart. Now it epitomizes nothing more than betrayal and misplaced trust.

Taking a shuddering breath, I pull my car onto the road and drive away. Forcing away my trepidation and gathering my self-worth, I remind myself my future is ahead of me and mine to claim. Because what forty-one-year-old woman doesn't relish the prospect of suddenly becoming single? Oh, and jobless with limited earning potential.

Like so many men, my husband Lawrence had a midlife crisis, but instead of buying a sports car or jumping from an airplane, he had an affair with his intern. His very young and naïve intern. I doubt she's much older than our children. She arrived on my doorstep this morning, begging me to let him go, because they were in love and desperate to be together. It took thirty seconds for my shock to clear and anger to erupt. When she rubbed her very rounded belly, the treachery kicked in.

How dare that weasel use me as an excuse!

I brought her inside, let her sob, cleaned up her mascara, and listened as she blubbered about how amazing Lawrence is. She's in for a nasty surprise, but as she'll never believe me, there's no point telling her. Who knows, maybe he does care about her. She seems to adore the ground he walks on, which will appeal to his inflated ego.

I agreed to surrender him to be her soul mate, her words, not mine. Blood coated my tongue as I held back my lecture about how soul mates just are. You can't be released to be one. Her gratitude, and I say her because I never caught her name, threw me a curve ball. I felt I was offering a tiny, fragile mouse to a lion to toy with before he mercilessly devours it alive.

While helping her pack an overnight bag for him, I tried dropping subtle hints that she could parent alone, but she heard none of it. I was not prepared to be cast as the evil wife, so I didn't push. Although friends, I was more than happy to take the role of the vengeful and slighted spouse and helped her 'clear out' the clothing she wouldn't want to see him in. His designer jeans, Italian loafers, bespoke suits and cherished 1930s tuxedo are all gone. It was petty, but I don't care. It was too satisfying. If he wants it back, he can trawl the charity shop it was donated to.

My tiny slice of retribution withered when I realized how little I had to my name. The house, most of our savings, the business are all his. Lawrence will not hand over a penny until forced to by a judge.

Not that there's any guarantee I'll be awarded much of anything else in the divorce. Especially as the comfortable lifestyle we enjoyed was courtesy of a stipend from old family money on his side. I never quite worked out how Lawrence's family had amassed their wealth or how much of it they had. Which will not help my case.

I transferred what I could to my personal account, and helped by Lea, my best friend for over ten years, I gathered the meager few items that were mine. She's one of the few people I trust, and her love of cloak and dagger espionage made her the perfect co-conspirator. That and her dislike for Lawrence. Together, we went through the house with a fine-tooth comb, ensuring I had everything that was mine. She even ran out and purchased me a new set of dark purple luggage as a celebratory gift. Told you she isn't a fan.

She's storing a few boxes for me and will ship them when I'm ready. Most of my worldly possessions, which mean anything to me, are loaded into my car. The one that I never wanted, mind you. I prefer smaller and more economical vehicles that are more practical around town. But Lawrence likes the status symbol of a label, including our cars, even the second one in the 'little wife's name'. I'm suddenly grateful he won, and picturing the smug, self-satisfied smirk tumble from his face when he realizes I was legally able to take it makes it all worthwhile.

The drive to my hotel for the night is blessedly quick, and within an hour, I'm alone in my room with my cases lined up by the door like soldiers ready for inspection. Any other time, I would have pulled out a book and relaxed on the sumptuous cream, leather sofa, but I have a future to plan and children to call.

Fearing the shock will ramp up the inner swirl of emotions that has tormented my life, I waste no time connecting my laptop to the hotel Wi-Fi and video call the twins without bothering to check the time.

Not that it will be an issue for Ruby, my daughter, she's what Lawrence indulgently calls a free spirit. I can think of better terms, but telling her it's time to buckle down and pick a life path is only met with hysterics from her and demands that I act with more compassion from Lawrence. She's twenty-two and on her third university course. Reminding them I was married with twins at that age does not help.

In stark contrast, Owen, her twin brother, is diligently studying to be a neurosurgeon on a full basketball scholarship in a top US college.

Their faces help ease the burning ache raging through my chest. Ruby rubs the sleep from her chestnut eyes and runs her fingers through her long auburn curls. I try to ignore how much like her father she is. Owen plonks himself on the ground, panting and covered in a sheen of sweat. The sounds of people shouting and a ball hitting the ground play out in the background.

"What's up, mum?" Owen, always my observant child, frowns into his phone.

"Wow, bro, how American do you sound?" Ruby sticks her tongue out.

"Hark, who's talking." He throws back, mimicking her crossed nationality accent. Lawrence and I are both half English and half American; the children have lived in both countries. I was raised in England by my English mother and Lawrence was mainly raised in the US, despite his parents being very British. They moved back to the UK about fifteen years ago.

"Your father and I are..." I can't bring myself to tell them. The words die in my throat and a tear threatens to roll down my cheek. I clasp my trembling hands together. No parent wants to deliver this news, and no child wants to hear it.

"Are what?" Owen prompts, his golden-blonde hair glinting in the bright Californian sun.

"Where's the pointing?" Ruby asks, referring to my overuse of hand gestures while talking and tips her laptop to see more of the image. A habit she hasn't lost since she was two, despite knowing it doesn't do anything.

"Separated." I manage and heave in a deep breath, waiting for their tears and despair. Ruby gawks, open-mouthed, shaking her head.

"Why?" Owen sits forward, scrutinizing me, his protector spirit very much on display.

"Umm..." I stutter, wishing I didn't have to tell them. Although, I wish for a lot of things, all the time.

"What did you do now, mum?" Anger floods into Ruby's accusation, and her eyes narrow to slits. I force myself not to react. It isn't her fault her father is her hero who can do no wrong. He worked hard to make her see him that way.

"I'm allowing your father to be free to marry his pregnant... lady friend." Somehow, I resist calling her the naïve mouse but suspect it'll stick in my head.

"I'm getting a baby sibling. I want a girl." I shake my head and slam my mouth shut to avoid screaming at my daughter.

"Seriously, Rue? Mum tells you dad got another woman pregnant, and you're happy?" Owen is the only person who never makes an excuse for her, not that anyone can blame him. Lawrence never really made any attempt to hide that he had a favorite. It makes—made for a tempestuous family life. I cannot cope with one of their arguments at the moment, though.

"Sorry." She says absently, trying not to let us see her texting her father.

"Sure, you are." Ruby ignores Owen's disgust. "I'm on your side, mum."

"There are no sides. Just two parents who are no longer together." I insist, rubbing my temple, as the mother of all headaches poises to make my life even more of a living hell.

I nearly left Lawrence too many times to count, but the roadblock that stopped me was dividing my children. He'll fight to stay in Ruby's life, but not Owen's. He even went so far as to suggest we took one each when I was packing one day. Both of my children deserve two parents. I didn't have a father when I was growing up. Dad, not that I have ever called him that, would randomly turn up every few years, turn our lives upside down, then disappear. I wanted better for the twins.

"What are you going to do? Do you have a lawyer?" I hold up my hand to stop Owen from going into full warrior mode.

"No, but I will." I say in my best 'mum' tone. "It's getting late here, so I'll let you both go. Love you, and stay safe."

I end the call as they tell me they love me, too, and flop back, wrapping my arms around my middle. My children may be twins, but there are few similarities between them. They don't even class themselves as the same nationality. Owen views himself as American, mainly because of his obsessive love of basketball. Ruby more or less rejected everything non-British when we set down roots in the UK. Until then, we moved between the two countries, but as the children got older, they needed stability and the consistency of one education system.

We decided to stay close to Lawrence's family, in the UK. At which point, my mother moved way up north.

The delight of telling his stuck-up, wanna-be aristocrat mother that her precious son has brought such shameful gossip to her door is almost enough to make me call her. But only almost.

Lea will give me all the gory details. Her mother moves in the same social circles as her and will gladly pass on every juicy detail. Neither of them is fonder of her than I am.

My phone glares at me from its perch on the coffee table, daring me to take the plunge and make my next call. The one I hope will give me a future worth claiming. Firming my resolve, I pick it up and dial.

"Ginny, how lovely to hear from you." My grandmother's warmth seeps through the miles. Her visits were always the highlight of my childhood, she cared for me, took me out, even smiled at me just because I was me. It was the only time I wasn't passed from sitter to sitter to give Mum some peace.

I've long since made peace with my crappy upbringing. My mum did her best, which wasn't very good, but it was still her best. I had hoped she'd be a better grandmother, but the twins barely know her.

"Hi, Gran." I stammer. We talk often but rarely see each other. She hardly ever leaves the island she lives on, and I've never visited it.

"What's wrong?" I hear her bangles jingle as she sits in a chair, her nails tapping the table. I suspect she knows. She always seems to know everything, always has. She turned up at the hospital when I went into labor, then at our house when I broke my leg when the twins were little.

"I thought I might come and stay." I close my eyes to ward off the fear she'll say no. The one time Lawrence offered to take us there, she made excuses but invited me alone. "It's just me." I quickly add.

"That would be lovely, my dear. My home has always been open to you. Are you staying long? Your Aunt Valeria needs help in her store." The genuine smile in her voice soothes my breaking soul.

"I was hoping to stay for a while. I'd love to help." Having something to fill my days will be a miracle. It isn't like I'll have anything else to do.

"Wonderful." The sudden booming bang of Gran clapping makes me jump, just as it always does. It's such an echoey, momentous sound. "Have you organized travel?"

"No," I sniffle and open my laptop to check flights, wishing I knew more about Whispering Isle. "What's the nearest airport?"

"I'll have to take care of that. You're coming from The Faraway." I'm told as though it's obvious. She has always called anywhere beyond her island home The Faraway. It only ever intrigued me more. "I'll email the details shortly. Do you have the necklace I sent you?"

I reach for the silver genie lamp pendant that never leaves my neck; it matches the one she wears. "Of course."

"Good, do not take it off before you get here." She warns, her tone darkening considerably.

"Okay. Why?" She was always mysterious and eccentric. Mum calls her kooky and then stares at me with an accusation. I take after my grandmother in many ways, particularly in looks. My bright blonde hair and azure blue eyes are all her. But I never inherited her free spirit, despite wishing I had.

"All in good time, my dear." I hear her shuffling around the house. "Right, I'm going to make travel arrangements. I'll be in touch soon."

"I'm sure I can arrange it." It's my secret talent, fuelled by my dislike of uncertainty and chaos. It churns the emotional swirling inside me. There's a heavy silence, and the seconds tick by, making me wonder if she's looking for a reason for me not to visit. My hope for a future to claim begins to fade.

"You can't." She says with finality to her words.

"I see." If she comes back to tell me I can't visit after all, I'll find something else.

"Genevieve," her sharp tone and use of my full name sends alarm bells thundering through my mind. "Do not make any wishes. Absolutely none." Her closing words leave me staring puzzledly at my phone, wondering what that meant.

One of my earliest memories is of my mother telling me to wish for everything, all the time, because nothing happens any other way. That set me down a path of wishes. So far today, I've wished about a million times my soon-to-be ex hadn't got someone else pregnant. That his dick would shrivel and fall off. That I had a career to fall back on and that I had been more sensible in securing my personal economic future. My children weren't so divided. The ten years we spent trying for another child had proved no more fruitful than just tests, and there was no reason why we didn't conceive. I even wished the naïve mouse would come to her senses.

Ever since Gran hung up, I've wished without even being aware of it that I had a glass of wine or a cup of tea and a box of chocolates. That's not to mention how I wished the dark clouds and the growling wind would vanish.

I check the room for a blanket to throw over my shoulders so I wouldn't have to find the energy to close the balcony door or turn the heating up and fail. Yep, I wished for one of those as well. A soft, thick, fluffy one in dark gray to suit my mood.

A knock at the door demands I drag my weary self to answer it.

"Room service, ma'am." A smartly dressed young man with bright ginger hair pushes a loaded cart in, laying a dark gray, fluffy blanket over the back of the sofa and another on the arm. He places a bottle of my favorite wine on the coffee table, along with the biggest box of my much-loved chocolates I've ever seen. As he closes the sliding door to the balcony, the clouds and wind clear away, revealing the twinkling stars in the night sky. He then fills the kettle and switches it on, checking that the tiny kitchen is fully stocked. Finally, he passes me the remote control for the heating panel and leaves with a bow.

My fatigued, bewildered brain refuses to process that chain of events or let me move away from my spot by the door. The kettle boiling is the catalyst I need to move.

I take my steaming mug, embossed with the hotel's logo, and sit on the sofa, wrapping myself in the fluffy blanket. Wishing my wishes really made things happen.

I remember how hard I wished I wasn't pregnant with the twins. I was eighteen, in college, and alone. With no idea how the American healthcare system worked, the bills were astronomical, especially for a Brit used to free healthcare. The doctor suggested I talk to the father, and soon, I was already five months gone.

Going home was not an option. My mother never wanted me, not really. There was no way she'd take me back pregnant.

I didn't have any way to message my father, even if I had wanted to. Gran might have asked me to live with her, but somehow, Whispering was not the right choice back then.

My only other family is Rose, my half-sister, and she's fifteen years younger than me. Who I should call to tell her what happened, but I'd rather delay the worry about her smothering Lawrence in his sleep, and I'm not sure I'm joking.

Lawrence was my only option, and young, naïve me just forced myself to fit the image he had for me. Housewife, mother, and personal errand runner.

All that aside because it's the past, and there is nothing about it I can change. I've made so many wishes that I know beyond any doubt they are not real and hold no actual power. There's no way they will start magically coming true.

A shadow of apprehension flits up my spine, bursting into my mind like a glittery firework, making me question my assumption. It's based on a lifetime's belief that magic isn't real when it actually is. A few years ago, the shocking truth emerged that wizards, witches, and even fae actually exist and are truly capable of magic. Real honest-to-goodness magic.

Everyone knows where they were when they found out. It's just one of those things that was seared into the memory of every person. I was listening to the radio, cooking dinner. I recall turning on the TV and watching people shift into huge wild animals as the most intimidating man imaginable calmly announced that essence people existed. His brief speech gave no details other than that the kismet gifted them their essence, and the Essence Authority led them. He was the eminence and in charge of it all.

The reporter asked what that all meant. He scowled at her and repeated himself. The poor woman froze. Had it been me, I'd have bolted. When something unidentifiable and terrifying flew through his eyes, I switched the TV off and put a towel over it.

The speculations about him and the EA, as it is apparently known, intensified to feverish levels while fear escalated unchecked. I never condoned how essence people were treated. Some were even murdered. Many had to flee their homes. It was shocking to see neighbor turn on neighbor. There are even some cases where a family has rejected one of its own. It was disgusting.

The situation has improved, and everyone is slowly starting to comprehend that the only actual difference is that we now know. Essence people have been around forever, at least as long as us ordinary people, but it was a secret they guarded closely and died to protect.

Gradually, essence people are slowly opening up about what they are. It's the modern-day equivalent of coming out of the closet.

My phone beeps with Lawrence's ringtone, and through nothing more than habit, I check it instantly.

`Dear, Ginny, I ordered you, a few things, I thought, you might want, because, I'm considerate, like that.`

Anger bursts through me, and I clench my fists to stop myself from throwing my phone across the room.

A GENIE'S NEW START

Shame you weren't the type of considerate not to get someone pregnant. And no sentence needs that many bloody commas!

I then mute notifications for all communications from him and resolve to find a tough lawyer to deal with him and the divorce.

Huddling myself into a tight ball, I brace for the pain and betrayal to hit me like a sledgehammer. I've kept going all day, waiting for the moment I could fall apart. Now it's here.

I heave in deep breaths, letting go of my tightly bunched composure.

Nothing much happens. I'm not overwhelmed with remorse at the end of my twenty-plus-year marriage. There's no crushing devastation that another woman is giving my husband the baby I couldn't. I don't have an all-consuming longing to return to the house I called home. I don't even have any oppressive fears that my future will be a bleak, desolate path to a lonely old age.

A slow smile curves my mouth upwards as a lighter, brighter mood seeps into my core. I cast a glance at my new fancy luggage, my bare ring finger, and savor the unexpected moment of peace.

Starting over at forty-one will be what I make it because the future is mine to claim in any way I want.

Two

The crystal clear blue water of the Pacific Ocean glimmers before me, inviting me in. Although, as I'm on a ferry sailing somewhere between Hawaii and Whispering Isle, it probably isn't a great time to go for a swim. My journey has been more of a holiday, especially considering the infidelity that started it. I spent two nights in my hotel then had a stopover in California, where I had dinner with Owen, who is spitting mad at his father. Ruby is otherwise loving life. After a few days in Hawaii, I'm on the last leg of my voyage, a four-hour cruise to the island that only happens once a week. I'm refreshed and relaxed. If this tropical and enchanting lifestyle is a taste of my new life, I can't wait to claim it.

A GENIE'S NEW START

I suspect not having anyone to answer to or think about helped. No making sure dinner was ready or clothes ironed, and as for early starts, nope, not a chance. Switching off the incessant alarms that wrecked every single morning because Lawrence was incapable of waking up was a joy that I celebrated over a hotel breakfast. It would have been more pleasurable had I thought to do it the night before and slept an extra hour, but you can't have it all.

The steady thrum of conversation plays through me, adding to my excitement. The ferry looked tiny as it approached but seemed to expand as it got closer to the shore, and now that I'm aboard, it's spacious. There's even a relaxing, air-conditioned restaurant that offers a bewildering selection, everything from tacos to whole racks of ribs. Some people have already placed orders, and it isn't even ten am.

I nab a table with a huge parasol on the deck. Thankfully, I don't need to cart my luggage around with me, it's all taken care of. I had planned to read, but I'm too busy drinking in the atmosphere. I can't pinpoint how I'd describe it, somewhere between serene, exhilarating, and carefree. I can't get enough.

The array of people basking in the late morning sun is mind-boggling. Gran warned me the inhabitants were a varied lot, and she was right. A formidably tall, wafer-thin man with long, shiny, silver hair stands to the side, watching over everyone. Nodding greetings or examining you so intently you're left wondering if your knickers match your bra. I know this because that panicked thought flew through my mind when it was my turn for his intense scrutiny. I nodded a friendly greeting, but he didn't react.

A father runs after a toddler set on causing mayhem while his wife tends to the baby, taking the odd photo. I can't help but grin at the familiar scene. Only it was me chasing Owen while Lawrence showered Ruby with devotion. My eyes round as the father and son combo have a growling contest that's far too realistic. They high-five as the kid gets an ice cream with the promise to sit still with it.

My gaze remains on the family for a few more moments and then wanders to another. I watch, trying not to frown, because I could have sworn it was parents and children, but they all appear to be about the same age. The parents, because I can't stop thinking of them in any other way, are no older than Owen and Ruby, and their children are possibly late teens.

"Is this seat taken?" A smartly dressed, older woman with a shock of light brown curls and a twinkling grin asks.

"No. I'm alone." I grimace. "That's not something I should admit to."

"No, it isn't, but we're all Whisperians, you're safe." Her chuckle has an appealing melodic twinkle. "What takes you to the island?"

"What gave away I'm not a local?" I tease, tapping my finger on the side of my mouth. My English accent gets stronger whenever I'm in the US, always has. "I'm visiting my grandmother and helping my aunt with her shop."

"Oh, you're Ginny." She says, to my shock. "Everyone, this is Ginny."

A round of hellos and greetings rings out around me. I wave back timidly.

"Don't mind us, youngin." Wow, when was the last time anyone called me young? "Everyone knows everyone on Whispering, and your gran has been full of your visit for weeks." I let her slip of the tongue go. Despite usually taking years to warm up to most people, I'm instantly at ease with her.

"I'm looking forward to seeing the Island. I couldn't find anything about it online." In fact, I'd half expected to get to the dock this morning and find something waiting to fly me back to England.

"It's... secluded." She says, exchanging a knowing look with an older gentleman in a sharp three-piece suit, who sits in an empty chair at our table.

"One might even refer to it as enchanted." He agrees, staring adoringly into her eyes. It's great to see romance isn't dead, but after a few moments, it gets awkward.

"Oh, my! I haven't introduced us. I'm Hattie, and this is my husband, Herbert. We're in the same coterie." She extends her hand, and I shake it, admiring her firm grip.

"Coterie?" I ask, shaking Herbert's. He falters, his face falling.

"Let's have an ice cream. Ginny?" Hattie gets to her feet, eager to shuffle away.

"I'll get them. I was just thinking I could use something to cool off." I head to the lone refreshment stand with their requests, as unease at their relief floods through me. I've heard the term coterie before, but for the life of me, I can't place it.

My genie's lamp necklace must have been in the sun because it warms against my skin. I lift my hand and move it outside my dark blue mini sundress. One of my many Hawaii purchases to celebrate wearing what I want.

Feeling an intense pull, I gaze up and into the marble gray eyes of a menacing behemoth of a man with hefty muscles showcased in a tight black t-shirt. I swallow the wow that threatens to burst from me. I've never had a bad boy thing, never understood it, but this gentleman, and I have no idea how loosely I'm using that phrase, is the most beautiful specimen I've ever seen. My fingers itch to explore the lines of black ink adorning his colossal arms, and I imagine most of his perfect physique.

"What can I get you?" The terse question rips my attention to the haggard server, her scowl stretching to her beady, bird-like eyes.

"Three 99s, please."

"Three what?" She snarls. Something sure crawled up her rear.

"Sorry, I forgot where I was. Ice creams, vanilla." I fan my heated face and resist the urge to gawk at his chiseled features.

The server rolls her eyes and hands me three cones stacked high with frozen confectionery. I pay one handed, fearing I'll drop them.

By the time I look up, he's gone, leaving me to wonder who my cutie is. I can't help but chuckle at what has apparently become my nickname for him because he was cute in the drop-dead-sexy, can-probably- okay, definitely-go-all-night-and-still-make-breakfast way. But nothing about the danger he radiated was cute.

"This is good ice cream." I practically groan while trying to hold on to some dignity, but, honestly, think of the best ice cream you have ever had and times it by a thousand, this is still better.

"It's from Whispering." Hattie sighs, her face mirroring mine. "All the food there is out of this world. Visit as many of the restaurants and eateries as you can. There are loads of them dotted all around."

Herbert drags his eyes from his wife's enjoyment to me. "Do you know anything about the island?"

"Apart from presuming the weather is good, no, not really." Absolutely nothing is closer, but admitting Gran never told me anything about her home is embarrassing. Hattie and Herbert grin at each other with all the excited contentment of someone who has been given full rein to regale you on their favorite subject.

"The streets are lined with fruit trees, almost every type of fruit is growing somewhere, all year round, and it's all for anyone to pick as they want. No one ever buys it, there is no need. Those in Charmedy are the best." Hattie tells me with authority.

"You are biased," Herbert chuckles at her. "Correct but biased. Charmedy is where we and your gran live and is the very southerly point. Do not tell everyone, but the best eating places are really there, but we keep them quiet. No need for the horde to know."

"Herbert," Hattie rolls her eyes at him. "Few except those who live there visit Charmedy, they find it too hicaldy picaldy. To the north of us, everything more or less runs across the island in straight lines, boring as that is. But, anyways, nearest us is Storeholder Row. Where the store holders all live, and, obviously, the stores."

"They are close to the stores," Herbert insists, suddenly growing very serious. "They all care for them properly."

"I'm certain they do." I reassure him, with no idea why it's an issue.

"The stores are mainly in their own row. They like to be together, for support and security. A few have strayed, but I'm sure they'll come back." Hattie supportively squeezes my hand across the table. I send her an encouraging smile.

"What's north of that?" I cannot even try to explain it, but talking about the shops sends unease tramping down my spine.

"Main Town, it sort of holds its own charm." Herbert waves dismissively in the air.

"Some districts are really quaint." Hattie gives him a loving but stern stare that does nothing to chase away Herbert's disdain or how it ignites my inner swirling. "You're merely not fond of the orderly approach the packs or the magicals have."

Herbert raises an eyebrow at her and carries on before I can fully digest what was said. "The harbor where we'll dock is on the outward curve side by the hotel."

"Outward curve? Isn't the island round?" The image of the perfect circular island has been with me since I was a toddler.

"No, dear, it's like a crescent moon. What made you think it was round?" Herbert frowns indulgently at me.

"I'm not certain." Something deep and troubled inside me screams that he's wrong. With great effort, I cast it aside.

"Then by there is the hotel and parks, pavilion and funfair. All the leisure and fun anyone could ever need. The absolute best place to hear live music." Hattie tells me earnestly. "The acoustics are perfect."

"A fresh spell each time. The funfair likes to mix it up as well." Herbert's grin slips away, leaving a stark warning splashed across his features. "You won't need to go further north. Ever."

"But there isn't any reason to." Hattie adds so quickly my head spins. "Going down the inward curve are all the beaches. North Beach is great for families, the show line is less sloped. Then South Beach is the nicest, the sand is softer, water bluer, and it leads to Flowing Woods, which are the prettiest you can see. Honestly, every type of flower you could hope to see."

"How does it all fit? I thought the island was tiny." Maybe the shock of my marriage ending or the jet lag has caught up with me because bits and pieces of what they've said keep flashing in my mind. Pack, magicals, spells, and how huge it all sounds.

"It's Whispering, my dear, what has size got to do with it?" Hattie says, as if that answers my question. "The sunrises on South Beach are to die for, you absolutely must see it at least once."

I promise to see the sun rise from South Beach and listen as they continue to regale me with more details of Whispering, and I cast my gaze around us again. This time, observing each person in more detail. The family is definitely just that, despite the parents looking the same age. The father and son combo howling is just too good at it. A burly man huddles a woman with a stunning silver-blue hue to her skin against his chest. When I catch the eye of the tall, wafer-thin man, they change to something else entirely. It isn't scary but definitely not human.

I reach for my genie lamp necklace as reality bites my consciousness with a ferocity that steals my breath and sends my heart rate rocketing.

"The best thing about Whispering is the people who call it home." Herbert puts his hand on my lower arm resting on the table, grounding my wayward, spiraling thoughts.

"That's good." I truly want to believe him because no one on the boat is an ordinary, non-essence person except me. Which is fine, I tell myself. They are still normal people. Who can turn into wild animals capable of killing me or have magic that can...? What? What can magic do? I don't have a clue!

"Remember, do not go into Obscurity Forest or near the vampires." Hattie warns me coldly, watching a man sitting at another table with collar length hair so dark it absorbs light. He oozes class, culture, and dangerous, raw sex appeal. Without interrupting his intense conversation, his attention swoops to us, and he smirks, tipping his head. I swallow the needy murmur in my throat.

I considered my cutie a bad boy, but he's got a lock-up-your-daughters vibe. This bloke has entombed-the-whole-family-in-the-panic-room thing going on.

What the hell is wrong with me? I don't swoon or want to jump into bed with random strangers, yet, I've wished I could twice in the past few hours.

I turn back to Hattie and Herbert, who pointedly stare at my Adonis as he stands and heads inside. He's accompanied by another vampire wearing a burgundy, velvet suit with elaborate brocade gold embroidery and matching breeches that he somehow manages to pull off. His grin is nothing but congenial.

Adonis is not the most original nickname, but at least it's not stud muffin. I bestowed that on George Clooney.

Not ready to leave my prime spot, I decline Hattie and Herbert's invitation to join them for lunch.

My phone beeps with Owen's message tone. I take a deep breath as I debate checking it. The divorce lawyer he found has recommended hiring someone to investigate my husband's family wealth. I promised him I would carefully consider it, which I kind of have. By that, I mean I haven't been able to find a single reason why his family's financial situation is relevant to our divorce. I want my fair share of our assets, nothing more. Lawrence's lawyer is already playing hard ball and putting obstacles in the way, finding out what that is will not be easy. It'll be buried deep, away from prying eyes. My shoulders fall as that thought hits home with the force of a sledgehammer.

His mother loves to drop hints about an aristocratic background and showing off her latest extravagant purchases. Everything has to be top of the line, prestigious, and easily recognizable, but she is always quick to explain it was a bargain. Either she had the Midas touch to finding a sale, or something is going on.

I put the thoughts from my mind and pull my new e-reader from my bag. I left most of my physical books behind. Some, mainly the signed ones, went with Lea. The rest are still at the house or wherever Lawrence sent them. Moments before seeing it, I was staring into a bookshop thinking about my lost volumes, wishing I had a never-ending supply of books wherever I am. Now I do. I settle down, picking a title at random.

It isn't long before the smell of food proves too much to ignore, and my stomach is rumbling for lunch. I was running late this morning, one of my worst habits, and barely managed an orange juice before I had to head to the marina.

After a delicious chicken and bacon salad and fruit juice eaten inside, I head back out. My table is occupied by a group playing cards. Their boisterous game looks fun, and I'm sure I'd be welcome to use the spare chair, but for the moment, I prefer something calmer. I wander around the deck, finding a tranquil spot at the back of the ferry with plentiful shade and comfy loungers.

I take a seat, resting my chin on my knees as I hug them to my chest, bracing myself for a bout of grief, betrayal, and all the good stuff to come and hit me. I've done this several times over the last week, but, yet again, the only thing that slaps me with brute force is how much of an idiot I was for staying after the twins were in university. Before then, I can justify my choices, not easily, but I can.

The last week has been an eye-opener, a proverbial palette cleanser for my life. It's amazing how differently you perceive things after you lose it. Hardly any of my clothes are what I packed, my staid, dour wardrobe is currently gracing charity shops and thrift stores on both sides of the Atlantic. My new style is brighter, lighter, and unbelievably more comfortable.

I stretch out, realizing that looking at where we've come from makes moving forward more authentic. My daughter's ringtone steals my moment of introspection. I answer, bracing myself. She doesn't tend to listen to voicemails or check messages and may still think I'm in the UK.

"Garlic, really, Mum, Garlic." I roll my eyes at her indignation and conceal my chuckle. I'd forgotten I told the naïve mouse that Lawrence loved garlic but wouldn't eat it as he was worried about kissing with garlic breath. He hates it. Another petty act of vengeance.

"Hello, Ruby, it's lovely to hear from you. I've had a good journey. Thank you for checking up on me." I cut in.

"Journey? What journey?" She says. I switch my camera on and stand to show her the pacific ocean. "You went on holiday? Mum, there's a baby on the way."

I flop against the railing, shaking my head and open my mouth to speak, but I have no words.

"Don't you want to be there for Dad?"

"What?" I gawk, dumbfounded. She can be totally oblivious to how anyone else feels, but this is ridiculous.

"Don't you want to be there for Dad?" She says as if talking to a two-year-old with learning difficulties. My finger hovers over the end call button as a gust of wind blows the phone from my hand into the deep water below.

"No!" I cry. Nausea rolling through me. My life is on my phone, all my numbers, passwords, everything.

From nowhere, someone dives overboard. I scream and dart around, searching for a way to sound the alarm. Within seconds, my cutie rises from the water and lands on the deck.

Without my permission or conscious thought, my hand lifts and runs down his chest, testing his shirt. He should be dripping wet, but he's bone dry.

"Your phone, ma'am." His smooth, crisp voice is like honey for the ears, making me want to lap up every syllable.

"You're dry." I marvel, savoring the hard muscles of his solid chest.

"Yes, ma'am." His second ma'am worms its way through my naughty moment, and I yank my hand back. "It's an essence thing..."

"Please do not call me ma'am again." I nearly beg, finally taking my dry phone from him. There's nothing like having the hot man you were wishing would ask you out talking to you like you're his mother's age.

"Sorry." He grins. Had he not dropped the preverbal bucket of cold water over my libido, I would have blushed because his grin would leave my stud muffin to shame. He holds his hand out. "Draven."

"Ginny." His calloused palm rubs my skin, and I daren't imagine the effect they would have on the rest of my body.

"Mum!" My daughter's voice screams through my phone. Draven nods and steps away.

"Sorry, I dropped my phone and..."

"Of course, you did." She huffs just as she does when she's about to run to Lawrence because I had the audacity to tell her no. "Anyone would think you don't want to know about the baby."

"Because I don't. Your father had an affair with a girl barely older than you and got her pregnant then tried to use me as an excuse for not standing by her. In no way, shape, or form do I want to hear about it." I bite my tongue to stop my rant.

"I see."

"Good. How are you?" I try, aiming for a normal mother-daughter conversation.

"Well, I can't tell you about the biggest thing to ever happen to me, can I?" Her whine is meant to make me feel guilty.

"No, do you have anything else to say? Like asking how I am in the shadow of my husband's betrayal or how my journey was?"

"S'pose." She grumbles, crossing her arms and pouting.

"Well, I'm picking up the pieces and moving on with my life. The journey was lovely. Thank you for your interest." I take deep breaths in the hope of regulating my temper. "How are you?"

"Fine."

"Good, I need to get a drink. I'll call you in a few days." I hang up, ignoring her outrage. My head falls back, and I press the bridge of my nose with my thumb and forefinger. Then put my phone back in my bag and go inside.

"You look like someone who needs a good dose of sugar." The matronly server declares as her ample bosom struggles to stay contained behind the poppers of her red polyester tunic, which must be sweltering.

"That sounds perfect." I point to a divine chocolate cake and order two slices and two sodas. My cutie, who now needs a nickname more suited to someone who has mum-zoned me, deserves something as a thank you.

I find him reclining in one of the loungers, relaxation making him even sexier.

"A thank you. I hope you like cake and soda."

"Thanks." He hesitantly takes both, swallowing hard, his Adam's apple bobbing. A shield falls over his features, losing the semi-eased thing he had going on a moment ago.

"I'm going to see if I can find a table." I wave, walking away, pretending I didn't see his relief, quickly nabbing a tiny table and lone chair on the shady side of the boat. Where I can soak up the animated chatter of other passengers. The cake is every bit as good as it looked, and all too soon, my sublime, edible mood-booster is gone.

There's something extra calming about being out of the searing heat, not least of which is the decreased risk of sunburn. A serious consideration when you're pasty white. I'd love to achieve the healthy glow of a tan, but I either go bright red after thirty seconds or barely manage a delicate shade of pink all day. My hair, though, always goes a brighter, more fake-looking shade of blonde. Oh, and unmanageably frizzy. No matter what treatment, oil, or conditioner I use, it's always the same. I look like someone stuck a huge, tacky halo on a bottle of milk.

Plus, I'm constantly molting. If I sit somewhere for more than a couple of moments, I leave stray hairs behind. Even now, I pick one from my dress and let it go on the wind. Owen, my gran, and my sister have beautiful golden locks that are always flawless and tan to a golden perfection.

Two women walk past, one digs through her bag and shakes her head. The other snaps her fingers, and they're both wearing sunglasses. My concept of normal and rational is going to take one hell of a pounding. I truly detest not knowing what to expect, and Whispering is a mystery. The more I find out about it, the deeper the unknown.

Three

Vibrant excitement cascades around me, filling the air with potent joyous energy. A thrillingly welcoming warmth shoots up my spine and explodes into my mind with a sense of belonging. I get to my feet because sitting still is impossible and pace to the front of the ferry.

I stand at the back of the hushed crowd and gaze upon the awe-inspiring, glimmering, dome-shaped rainbow that stands before us as a guardian of all within its protection. From a distance, it appears to be almost nothing but a trick of the light, but as we approach, its reflective properties reveal it as glass. Alarm shoots through me, and I step back against a solid chest. Hands wrap around my arms, securing me in place. It may not be painful, but his grip isn't gentle.

"Do not fear. It is merely the kismet powered barrier to shield the inhabitants from harm." The cultured, age old voice can only belong to my Adonis, the vampire I glimpsed earlier. The one I was warned to stay away from.

"But it's glass." I stammer, fearing it will crack and shatter.

"Shh, just wait." Warm breath cascades down my neck as he whispers in my ear. "You are very safe. Just enjoy"

His hands move down my arms and onto my waist. The urge to tilt my head and expose my neck flees my mind as the ferry breaches the iridescent armor that stretches as far as the eye can see. I pull back and closer to Adonis.

The luminous light person as we sail through. When it reaches me, I lift my hands and wondrously marvel at the intoxicating euphoria and breathe.

"See, you are most secure." Then he's gone. I dart around, but he's nowhere in sight. Only my cutie scowling at a closing door to my side.

The feeling of being home curls through me as I'm engulfed in Gran's floral scent and loving embrace. Her bubbly, joyful energy permeates the gulf of misery that has made my inner swirl of emotions home.

"I am so glad you're finally here, Ginny." My gran holds me at arm's length, scrutinizing every inch of me. "You're looking good."

"Thanks. I feel like I've had a holiday." I give her a teary but happy smile.

"That's how it should be." She tells me sincerely, her brow pulled tight. She's rarely serious, and it always struck me as not really her. "Let's get you home."

"That would be good." We link arms to make our way up the broad walk, the ferry once again appearing much smaller. Vessels from tiny row boats to luxury yachts bob around on the gentle tide. The air is clear, perfumed, and soothing.

The baggage claim is in a small white building with a red pitch roof and large open doors. People mill around, waiting for their luggage, making the most of the air conditioning and huge ceiling fans.

My cases are to the side with Hattie and Herbert, who call us over. I thank them and reiterate my promise to see the sunrise from South Beach.

"You must be Ginny. I'm so excited to finally meet you and get the store open again." A robust young woman wearing an eye-watering, neon green jumpsuit jumps at me with startling enthusiasm. Her too-firm handshake pumps my arm, slightly jarring my shoulder. The joys of aging, you don't get to shake off such things anymore, instead, they stay with you for days.

"Great. And you are?" I ask, looking way up because she's well over six feet, probably nearer seven, and broad. Many men would love her frame, and most women would be awkwardly trying to cover it up, but she owns it, and I already adore that.

"Deloria, but everyone calls me Delly. Don't look now, but Draven is looking this way." Her eyes round as they sweep his frame before shooting to the left and widening. "Girl, you had the ferry ride of a lifetime. Draven and Eragon."

I follow her eye line and see my Adonis staring intently at us, framed by a doorway on the island side. The blackness of his suit and hair casts dark energy that shrouds his body, at odds with the bright flora and fauna surrounding him. Yet, emphasizes the sinister, blood-red brightness of his cravat and eyes.

"They seem nice enough." I shrug.

"Delly, let Rubaline and Ginny be, sweetheart." Herbert corrals her away with an apologetic bow to Gran, who regally waves them off.

A short man with impossibly huge biceps and very little neck pulls up in a golf cart style vehicle and stands to attention by the side of my purple cases. "Where to doyen Rubaline."

"The house for Valeria's store, Jerry." He loads everything and takes off at speed. "I considered it would be best if you stayed there."

"Okay, but I thought I was simply helping her." I'm a bit hurt not to be staying with Gran. It's been one of my dreams since I was tiny.

"She is taking a break, a holiday if you will." Gran twists her lips, whirling her finger in the air, roughly pointing in multiple directions. I'm used to Gran in long, flowing skirts in an array of bright colors, not the business-like, royal blue skirt and jacket she has on. It's taking some getting used to. "We'll take scooters. They are the main mode of transport on Whispering."

She leads us to a stand of bright yellow electric scooters. Gran taps a card twice and pulls two out. After a quick lesson on how to use it, Gran takes off, and I have no option but to jump on and follow. Once I'm used to it and realize the wide wheels mean they aren't as wobbly as I'd feared, they are a lot of fun. Now I get why the twins spent hours chasing each other around the back garden, not that theirs were electric.

We take a coastal path overlooking a steep drop into rough water. The lack of barriers should scare the daylights out of me, but I feel safe and protected.

I glance at the cheerful, fruit tree-lined streets with an astounding variety of properties, many are festooned with flowers. People greet each other, including us, with friendly waves. The total lack of rushing around and stress makes it all seem perfectly peaceful and tranquil, just like the calm before the storm.

There are no cars, not a single one, and no traffic noise interrupts the birdsong and trees swaying in the breeze. The roads are wide enough and paved, but there's no separate space for people to walk, and no one bothers to look when they step out of their front gate.

"It is very special, isn't it?" I nod at Gran, sighing dreamily. If this is the future I'm here to claim, it will be nothing but idyllic.

A niggle clicks to life, reminding me that if something seems too good to be true, it probably is. I look deeper. Sure, the shadows seem too obscure to match anything that could cast them, and tiny figures frantically scramble from one hiding place to another. I catch the eye of one as he or she, I cannot be certain, peers out from behind an apple tree. It scurries away before I react.

We arrive in a long street of more formal houses, many with a corporate vibe I didn't expect. We slide the scooters into the stand, and Gran taps her card twice against a tiny screen.

"We'll sort your card when we know if the store will accept you." Before I question what she means, she turns, lifting her arms, moving backward with a flourish, jingling her array of bangles. People step outside, either openly watching us or trimming a manicured bush in their front garden.

"These are the store holder houses. Look after the store, and the house will look after you." Gran points to a house with darkened windows and cracked paint. "See what I mean?"

"Not really." I shake my head, trying to chase away the unease attempting to creep into me. She rolls her eyes and walks the way we came, stopping outside the last house on the street, a stone's throw from the steep cliff.

"This is the house for the Emporium." Her grandiose tone does not match the quaint, pale blue cottage with white trim and country garden, complete with pots overflowing with herbs and raised vegetable beds. Gran watches me, seeing into my soul, stripping me of pretense and bearing my vulnerability. "How does it feel?"

"Like a place to protect me from the scrutiny of a thousand and one eyes gawking at me." I mutter quickly, walking up the invitingly tranquil path and through the partially open door. Gran follows me in, closing the door with a reassuring click.

"That is a good sign." I ignore her eyes boring into my head and kick my shoes off. "How does the house feel now?"

"Like a house?" I'm not sure what she's after from me.

"Evil? Charming? Content? Malevolent? Murderous? Productive? Sunny? Cold?"

I hold up my hand to stop her, fearing she will list every adjective until I give her something.

"It's charming, possibly a bit lacking in personal details and like it needs to warm up." I take a second to debate if I need to add more. "The welcoming invite I experienced outside has paled now I'm inside."

"To be expected, very much expected, but not unexpected. Don't you agree?"

"Yes?" I hope that's the right answer because my head is starting to pound, and my nerves have taken a nosedive. Something feels off, but reality never matches the aspiration.

"The tour." Gran twists around, searching high and low for something. She opens the door to the left and checks what's inside. "Downstairs half bath."

"That's handy."

She heads right through a sliding barn door. I have always wanted one. "Ahh, the sitting room."

The bright and airy space has silvery blue walls with soft lilac accents and an ornate floral wallpaper decorating the ceiling. Giving it a homely sense of luxury and style.

"It's stunning." I long to lie on the tempting sofa with a good book and mug of tea.

"Good, good." My gran's new habit of repeating her words does not seem to be vanishing. She pushes open pocket sliding doors, something else I've wished for. "The kitchen and dining room are combined."

I eagerly follow her into a kitchen that is a chef's dream. Big, shiny, chrome appliances sit majestically framed by pale gray quartz worktops that have a hint of sparkle. Plentiful shaker-style cabinets run the length of the walls, adding to the spacious atmosphere.

The island has seating for four people and a wireless phone charging point.

I can't wait to cook something. I love to cook and bake. I may not be the best, but that has yet to dampen my love for it. As long as what I produce is edible, is good enough for me. The table is an extendable beechwood masterpiece with ornate carving around the edge. The seat at the head of the table, overlooking the neat back garden, beckons me. I pull the chair out and sit.

"Home," springs from my mouth.

"Well, that is better." My gran surveys me for a moment, unpacking a new electric kettle - water boiled any other way just isn't the same - and plugs it into a perfect little nook for making tea and coffee, complete with a filter tap.

Gran gives me a steaming mug and a slice of carrot cake she retrieves from the fridge, which looks too delicious not to devour. Although this needs to be my last treat for some time, or the middle-aged spread I've sort of managed to avoid will take up residence in the wrong places.

"You may notice information appearing in your mind," my gran says, rolling her mug between her fingers. "That is normal and another good sign."

"A good sign of what?"

"That the store will accept you. How else will you help your aunt?" Had she paused for breath, I would have had a few more questions about being accepted by the store, but she didn't.

"You'll need staff. Delly was very... enthusiastic, if you don't mind the odd breakage. But only as a subordinate, she'll never be more, but few are."

"I expected the store to be up and running, and I was merely helping. It sounds like I'll be managing it. I know nothing about being a shopkeeper." A list of potential chores flies through my mind, churning my emotional swirl. "To be honest, this is more than I anticipated it would be. So much more. All of it, not only running a business, but..."

"Moderate the discombobulation, Ginny." My gran's hand covers mine, and I gulp a breath as my inner swirl slows and eases. "We can work on that if you would like."

"Yes, please." I return her triumphant grin with a somewhat confused one.

"We can get your card from the town hall now."

"Great." I pick up my plate and start eating. No one rips me away from yummy cake.

Four

The journey to the town hall takes us through a maze of streets with brightly-colored, artsy cottages with generous porches and tuneful wind chimes. The flower-festooned gardens have hand-crafted sculptures making each uniquely bohemian.

I get a kick from uncannily anticipating which turn Gran will take, but I wouldn't like to find my way through the twists and turns alone.

We soon arrive outside the imposing, red brick-built town hall. Its cream columns stretch to the sky, even though the building is no more than a few stories. The revolving glass door rotates at its own leisurely pace, despite the throng of people coming and going. My gaze zeroes in on a massive Bengal tiger casually ambling toward Gran and me.

"That's Logan. He's a clerk and good to the coterie, so stop looking like you're about to have a panic attack. Anyone would think you've never met a shifter before." My gran huffs, reminding me of Ruby.

"I haven't, at least not in this form." I try with all my might to stay put but take a step back, then another. The creature is massive, easily two hundred pounds, with huge paws and sharp teeth that could rip me to shreds in seconds.

"You'd better get used to it." My gran points up the street, and there are loads of animals walking in and out of a wooded area. Most shift into people and wave to Gran, but some wander off, still in their animal form. "Provided it isn't a full moon, you'll be fine."

"And if it is a full moon?" Her answer is lost as Logan bounds over, purring. "Gran, he's purring. How?"

It doesn't have the sweet sound of a house cat, but it's adorable all the same.

"All shifter cats purr." Gran says, rubbing her hand through his thick ,dark orange and black striped fur. "He's harmless. Come and say hello."

I obey her order before I can fully process it. The deadly big cat brushes against me and winds around my legs, purring his heart out. I crouch down and the tiger rests his head on

A GENIE'S NEW START

my shoulder, sighing gently. Tentatively, I stroke his soft neck, muscles ripple below my palm.

"Wow. You are incredible, aren't you, boy?" I croon, rubbing my forehead against his.

"You would do well to remember, there's still a man inside that cat. If you wouldn't hold a stranger that close, maybe don't him." Gran stands with hands on her hips, and I pull away, noticing how close to my chest he was.

"He's not so scary." I admit, giving him a final tickle behind his ear before we put our scooters into the stand.

The interior of the town hall is sleek and modern, a complete contrast to the traditional exterior. It's as though we stepped through a portal to another dimension. Something digs into my feet, and I look down to see I'm wearing smart blue stilettos and a brown business suit with a white chiffon blouse.

"What the ever-loving bleep." I huff a confused breath because I did not say bleep. I do not swear often, but when I do, I sure as bleep do not say bleep. "What the bleep."

My gran laughs, patting my shoulder, and moves away from me. An officious short, round man wearing a bright yellow tailcoat, trousers, and waistcoat marches to me. His skin glows an ever brighter orange, and his scowl deepens with each step. All I can think of is an Oompa Loompa in a clown costume.

"Who dared to transgress in the sacred space?" His square eyes drill through my conscience, and I raise my hand. "Your card!"

"I've come to get one." I shrug, feeling bad that I didn't have something to put in his outstretched palm.

"No card! You have no card! Who saw you through the dome?" His zig-zag hair rising to stand on end.

"She came by ferry, Hector, like everyone else." Gran glowers at him and gestures at the staid, black trouser suit and starched white shirt, buttoned tight around her neck. "When did this preposterous magic start?"

"I implemented it last week. It gives the building the class this forsaken island is sorely missing." Just when I thought there was no brighter shade of orange, I'm proved wrong, and his eyes twist to a diamond shape. Forcing me to look away for fear of being hypnotized.

"Is that when you changed the building's interior?" My gran asks sweetly. Oompa Loompa swings to her with one hand on his hip and waving the other at her in a naughty child point. Her tone drops to icy with a boatload of menace. "Or is this a trial to see if the Committee approves and my email was mislaid?"

Oompa's skin fades to a sickly, lemony yellow. "There's no need for that. I am a Bureaucrat."

"You are one of several on Whispering, all of whom answer to the Committee. Would you like to change it back or put it to the vote?" My gran's presence wraps around me in a dream-like, ethereal way, and without considering why, I turn to her and stand straighter, waiting for her verdict.

"I stand by my changes. Town Hall is mine." Oompa stamps his foot. Several people gasp. My eyes look toward the marina, or the direction I think is right, as I ponder jumping on the ferry and sailing back to normality.

"So be it." Gran decrees, twirling her hands in a fancy motion. I wait with bated breath, my eyes darting around to see what's going to happen, and nothing. Not a bleeping thing.

"By the way, swearing in your head counts as well." A woman with huge, laughing amber eyes and a genially upturned mouth tells me quietly. "If you want to get out of here today before those two have another war of the Musical Mondays, ask for your correction and card."

"War of the Musical Mondays?" I whisper, watching Gran and Oompa standing off against each other like gunfighters in the wild west.

"And you might want to do that before he takes his agitation at your gran out on you because she's right and he hates it." I'm warned.

"Please, can I have my correction and card?" It's not until after I've spoken I realize I don't know this woman and there's no guarantee she's steering me in the right direction. Just because she feels like a long-lost friend does not mean she's not a mortal enemy.

"Yes, yes, of course. Of course." Oompa strides back to me. By this point, I can only hope the habit of repeating oneself is not contagious. He inspects every inch of me with a dissatisfied grimace. "You don't *do* anything."

"I'll have you know I do loads. I am not lazy." I deeply resent his accusation and will not stand for it.

"Clearly, you do loads, but you can't actually do anything." He shoos me away. "Just collect your card."

His dismissal claws into my self-doubts, making me feel undervalued, something I promised would not happen in the future I'm here to claim. My hackles rise, drowning out my common sense as it screams that no correction is a good thing.

"Do not write me off, you officious little man." I regret my outburst even before his skin springs back a bright, bright orange, and, bleep it, I'm repeating myself.

"Bleep," I hear several people around me mutter.

"Your correction then will be to fix Sal's store, to run it smoothly enough for the house to fully care for the storekeeper." I'm more resentful of the venom in Oompa's words than the correction. If the store is fixable, then it should be sorted without it being a punishment. "The rest of you have five hours community service."

Oompa turns on his patent yellow heel and storms away with enough sway to his hips to make a stripper proud.

"That was harsh. You'll need help." My amber-eyed new friend shakes her head, staring after him. "He hasn't assigned anything to be our community service, and helping a store is a benefit to the community. I could meet you there at 9 am Sunday?"

"That would be great, thank you." I hold my hand out, and we shake on our deal. "I'm Ginny."

"I know who you are. Everyone does. I'm Sera." With a wink, she steps to the side as a stream of people take turns shaking my hand and telling me their names. After the fifth, I forget them all, and after the twelfth, the faces blend into one, even those with silver and gold skin or pointy ears.

"That was a lasting first impression. We'd better get your card before anything bleeping else happens. Guess I'm helping as well." Gran puts her arms around my shoulder and guides me to a counter.

In a daze, I get my photo taken, height, weight, and thumbprint recorded. Then I'm given a lengthy questionnaire but told there's no rush. In the morning will be fine. Before I can mention that as I arrived today, the morning would be a rush, my card is placed on the desk, and the receptionist is gone.

Tapping my own card to access a scooter gives me a sense of purpose that far outweighs the insignificant action. I tuck it into the useful, zipped pocket of my dress that every item of clothing should have and set off home.

Later or tomorrow, I'll take a stroll to Sal's store to see how much work and what supplies will be needed. I want to make the most of the five hours I have of everyone's time. I might even bake something for everyone Sunday. I consider my baking and decide to buy, there's no need to subject them to my barely edible offerings.

I find my way back effortlessly, with Gran only correcting one wrong turn. The front door opening as I step foot on the path doesn't surprise me. However, Jerry, standing to attention in the entryway, does. I snort inwardly at my own stupidity for actually believing the fantastical drivel I've read about magical houses and shops.

"If you would like to choose a bedroom, I will take your luggage up, Merchant." Jerry bows.

"Thanks." I shuffle past him in the slither of space not taken up by his huge frame. "Please, call me Ginny."

It may sound strange, but staircases are my weakness. I have chosen houses because of them and have refused to go back to pubs because the staircase to use the bathroom wasn't pleasant. This one is amazing, wide, light, and airy. The actual steps are the ideal height and depth, and more of the blonde wood flooring peeks out either side of the carpet running down the center. I fall the rest of the way, head over heels in love with this house, before I've reached the top.

Five doors and a decision greet me, made all the more perplexing by Gran and Jerry's eyes boring into my back. For a moment, I'm paralyzed by hesitancy and confusion. I expel a long, slow breath, forcing my jitters aside. Visually, the doors are identical, six panels, painted white, with sparkling pull handles mounted on a crescent moon backplate. Yet, the choice of which will be mine is momentous and not helped by my whirling emotions. An overwhelming curiosity about what's behind each door and a growing sense of defiance at being forced to choose leaves me in a tailspin.

After an excruciating eternity of internally warring with myself, I wish for the answer, and I'm compelled to turn right. My hand pauses on the sparkly handle, and an undeniably prosperous vibe trickles up my arm, fading just before it reaches my shoulder.

The room is an exquisitely dramatic mix of deep purples and dark pinks, with a picture window letting loads of light in. The bed is massive, at least a king, with a thick, velvety comforter and firm pillows. Opposite, the wall mounted TV sits above an oak dresser. I kick my shoes off and let my feet sink into the plush, deep pile carpet.

This room is more mine than any other else I could imagine. It's drawn me into its heart and will provide me with a serene space to escape the demands of life. There's a chance it will refuse to release me, not that I want it to.

The master bath is a spa oasis. I stroke the shiny chrome taps and sigh in contentment, debating if I should use the claw-foot tub or generous shower with the handy seat before I go to sleep tonight.

The walk-in closet is massive and fully decked out with shelves, drawers, and hanging space. My luggage sits on little stands where it can't wreck the bed, and I don't have to bend to the floor.

"We'll put everything away and head out for dinner." Gran says, standing by my largest case. I pull the key from my zipped pocket and unlock them all. It takes moments to decide where my belongings go. The empty half of the closet serves as a stark reminder of the treachery that ended my marriage. I might be glad to be claiming my future, but it doesn't change the fact of my husband's betrayal.

I startle awake in the early hours, bring my knees to my chest, and heave in deep breaths. Fragmented bits of information scatter through the periphery of my awareness, many refusing to join as whole facts. I understand things I didn't know yesterday. Oompa is a goblin. The town hall can control how it looks on the inside but not the outside. The fruit trees are cared for by witches with special affinities for plants.

Twitchy and unable to stay still, I climb from between the soft cotton sheets, throw on shorts and a hoodie, and reach for my favorite running shoes. I do not jog often, but when I do, I lose myself to the pounding of my feet and the rhythm of music. However, if I do that today, I may not find my way back. I put on my comfy, velcro walking sandals instead. Who needs to be stylish, at? I check the time and growl when it's only half past four.

On the plus side, I can watch the sunrise from South Beach. Tired and deep in thought, I go into autopilot, cooking the entire pack of bacon. If there's anyone else around, they can share. If not, I have lunch and possibly dinner sorted. I plonk them and a big flask of steaming hot tea into a bag and head off.

The scooter stand is too tempting to ignore, and I zap through the deserted streets. Blaming the bright moon and twinkling stars illuminating the sky for the eery sensation, making the hairs on the back of my neck rise.

My gaze collides with a near-derelict, three-story, colonial-style house with a double garage and an overgrown formal garden with unpruned rose bushes. Not even the streetlight can penetrate the shadows, swathing it in a deathly cocoon.

In bleak contrast, the houses on either side are immaculately cared for. One a ranch-style with dark gray siding, and the other is a pale green craftsman cottage.

A pair of piercing, beady eyes peek from behind the closed curtains of an upstairs window. Nothing about the house hints it's occupied. Not wanting it to seem like I'm a crazed stalker or casing the joint, I carry on.

I park the scooter and stroll along the decking, dissecting the golden sandy beach with the rest of the island. Kiosks wait patiently to be opened and start serving customers. Seating and sunbeds sit unoccupied, all basked in moonlight. I find a spot where my sightline won't be obscured by any of the trees that will later offer shade against the heat of the sun.

The lack of light pollution offers a vivid view of the bountiful stars glistening in the night sky. I sip my tea, staring at them, hoping the reminder of how vast the universe is will help my mind settle. It serves as proof that everything has happened before and will happen again millions of times. Not necessarily in the exact same way, but spouses have been unfaithful for as long as there have been relationships. Children have left home since the creation of families. People have moved across land and sea since the birth of people. None of these are going to stop. With the passage of time, there will simply be a fresh batch of folks to make the same discoveries and mistakes.

I'm one of many. Thousands, possibly millions, who have taken the adventure of claiming a new life for myself. A soft roar sounds above me. I search the skies for the culprit, only glimpsing wisps of movement, almost as if something is effortlessly flying between the stars themselves.

Far out to sea, a large form nosedives into the water, barely disturbing the moon's reflection on the rippling waves. The figure shoots into the sky, opening broad, strong, reptilian wings and leaving a trail of smoke as he or she soars before diving into the sea.

Water dragon, one of the rare elemental dragons. Pops into my mind, and the queasiness that woke me up is back. More factoids wait to clamber into my head and burst to existence if I'm brave enough to let them in. The logic-based part of me screams to reject it, but my heart yearns for me to embrace everything.

The first rays of a new day dance with unrestrained abandon on the undulating waves of the receding tide. The glowing sun illuminates the sky, casting the infinite stars into unseen obscurity, concealing their unrivaled beauty behind a barrier of light that brings life and warmth.

There's a lesson there somewhere. Probably about the light overcoming the darkness, but, somehow, losing the majesty of the universe does not feel like a victory.

I tip my lukewarm tea away and pour a fresh one from my flask, watching the dragon repeatedly dive under the sea each time he flies higher and stays under longer. But I know he can stay below water for days, breathing as happily as he does on land. The daylight allows me to see his deep blue with mean spikes running from the top of his head to the very end of his tail.

An owl coos over my head, a shifter, because the sound is lower and more rumbly. A snake slithers across the sand, again, a shifter because the scales are almost perfectly round. Tiny tidbits about witches, wizards, fae, elves, and pixies are all floating around my bewildered, besieged head. All I can do is gawk unseeingly at a glorious sunrise.

"Hey, Ginny, you okay?" A familiar, deep, honeyed voice breaks through my melancholy panic. I nod, trying for reassuring, but when Draven sits on the edge of my lounger, tilting his head to see into my eyes, I'm certain I failed.

"I'm fine, honest." I force my tone to stay steady and, while his slightly raised brow tells me he isn't buying it, he moves to the adjacent seat.

I offer him a sandwich and munch one myself, giving me a moment to collect my thoughts.

"How come you're wet?" Tempting spheres of water saunter over the surging planes of muscled physique. If his body graced book covers, every author would be a bestseller.

He sheepishly looks down. "I didn't need to keep anything dry."

"Oh, thank you for keeping my phone dry. I have everything on it."

"You are welcome." Friends, if you could let me know how to stop staring at his abs, I'd be grateful. "Now, are you going to tell me what's got you all jittery?"

"I've been through a lot in the past week and traveled a long way to a strange land." I mean the last bit to sound humorous, but it comes out strangled. I flop back, raising my hands, pointing to everything. Draven tracks the movement. "Whispering is... unusual."

I want to say weird, bizarre, or freaky. They all somehow fit, which normalizes it all.

"It is very unusual. Not even Rock Falls holds a candle to the oddities here." He chuckles, laying back. The sun is already heating the air, despite the early hour.

"That's where the EA is based, right?" I question, making sure I have my facts right, but I can picture an intimidating building made with huge rocks set in a picturesque, small American town.

"For the US, yes, and where the eminence is. There are other bases all over the world." There's a respect hidden behind the wistfulness in his voice, and I twist to regard him carefully. His expression turns mournful for the briefest second before going blank. "It's a long story."

"They usually are." I offer him another sandwich and sit back to watch the sun sparkle on the waves.

"I heard a nasty rumor you have a correction of fixing Sal's store."

"I'm sure it just needs a good clean up and lick of paint, maybe some rearranging. I have plenty of help." I shrug.

"Rubaline hasn't explained much, has she?" I shake my head, not liking his hesitancy.

"Come by my sister's store about midday, and I'll take over while you two get lunch, and she can go through the basics."

"You would do that?"

"Sure. Besides, I don't have anything else." He runs his hands over his face and through his short, dark hair, but not before I catch his grief and hear his bitterness.

"Well, whatever the reason, I'm grateful. What shop am I looking for?"

"Paige's Book Bonanza." Draven shakes his head, sighing. "If you can't find your way through the maze of books, shout, and we'll find you."

"That bad?"

"For every one she sells, she orders three. I have no idea how she earns merits."

"Merits?" I presumed people here earned money. Gran paid cash for dinner yesterday, with no mentions of a merit.

"Nothing runs the same on Whispering. Paige will go through it."

"Right, of course. It's not the same. Why would it be the same?" My heart rate increases, and my body starts to flood with adrenalin as fractured images of previous storekeepers cascade through my mind. Some are elevated with enlightenment, while others have been cast aside to fade into obscurity. And I have no idea what that even means.

"You'll have help." Draven's calloused hand wraps around my arm, sending shivers flying through me.

"Great," I say with a very forced smile that he ignores.

"Has information started appearing in your head?" He asks me softly.

"How did you know?"

"It's normal." He gives my arm a final squeeze and stands.

"I'm not going mad?" The tension uncoils, and my swirling emotions ease their uncontrolled spinning.

"No, I promise, you are not going mad." He winks, and it's all I can do not to whimper. I'm a middle-aged, or nearly middle-aged, woman. I refuse to fawn over him like a teenager with her first crush. At least not in front of him

"Thank you." I praise myself for how normal I sound because he stands up wearing only a pair of short swimming trunks, bringing me to eye level with his muscular thighs.

"Would it be too strange for you if I shifted?"

"No, I'll avert my eyes." Although refraining from peeking behind my fingers might be a challenge.

"I'm not that detached." Draven grinds out as he shifts into the colossal sea-blue dragon I barely glimpse before he flies away. I let myself rummage through what I know, but nothing dings to explain Draven's reaction or how he shifted wearing his trunks.

Five

The sheer variety of shops is astounding. There's everything from quaint, old-fashioned shops to high-tech click-and-collect units. I deliberately came the long way around, to avoid going past my, or rather my aunt's, until I can give it my full attention.

Thinking about my, there I go again, my aunt's store throws me between wanting to flee from it and cherish it for eternity. I blow out a slow, frustrated breath. I am so done with having such conflicting emotions about everything.

Paige's store is central, and I'm confronted with a wall of books as soon as I enter. There's a narrow gap to the right that I can barely squeeze through.

After several turns, I end up back at the door. "Draven? Paige? How do I get through the maze?"

"See, I told you, you had too many books, sis," Draven grumbles. "Coming, Ginny."

"This way." A tall woman with Draven's eyes and aquamarine hair beckons me from the left. I follow her through an impossible-to-see opening to a checkout area, where I view bookshelves trailing through the deep space. "Dray, no amount of books is too many books. What am I meant to do, just let them go to a landfill?"

"They don't go to a landfill." Draven stares at his sister.

"They will not become compost." She cries, stroking a row of well-loved leather volumes with cracked, frayed spines.

"But customers can't get inside." He insists.

"And yet, here's Ginny." She links her arm through mine, guiding me through the maze, cursing when she knocks a pile of books over.

"I've got it." Draven's huff has more than a little growl.

"There's no need to be a grumpoid." She shoots over her shoulder, dragging me outside. I have to agree with Draven. That place is a death trap. The fire risk probably only outweighs the chances of being crushed alive. The air was also really musty.

"Sera will meet us in the Tavern. Draven is closing, not that he knows that yet." She gives out an evil mwahaha, then stops dead. "Damn, I forgot my purse."

We turn around, but Draven is behind us, holding it. "Do you want me to feed the kids as well?"

"See, you are a good brother. Don't get them hyped up on sugar, or I'll be sleeping somewhere else."

"No, you won't." He drawls.

"You're right, I'm not leaving my babies, but you'll be up with them." She grins, and he shakes his head. They have the type of easy, affectionate relationship I wished for the twins.

"Message me if you need a lift home," Draven calls as we walk away. I turn to wave and see him staring at my rear, his gaze lifts to my face, and he winks.

"How old are your babies?" Talking about children is a good way to drag my mind away from Draven.

"My boy is three. He's super lively and cute. My girl is five. She's got Draven's independent spirit, but you can't have it all." Paige pulls her phone from her purse and shows me photos of adorable children. My heart melts at their sweetness. We talk kids for the ten-minute walk to the pub.

The Tavern is dark, loud, and boisterous. Several pool tables take up the far end, with a dart board to the side. The long bar has a selection of barstools. Some seem safer than others.

"There are two main bars on Whispering. This is the one to drink without judgment. The other has a stuffy, country club vibe, which is fine for a date, but not when you want to laugh out loud. Wine, beer, or cocktails?" Paige walks straight to the bar, signaling a woman with huge dark eyes and a massive afro tied up by a stunning floral scarf.

"Draven called and got you a bottle of wine. Take a seat, and I'll bring it over."

"Join us if you get a break." Paige grins and tugs me to a comfy alcove seating in the corner with an oversized, low-hanging, ornate lamp that gives literally no light. "We'd better get the important bit out of the way."

"The store?" I pull a notepad and pens from my bag.

"More the relationship Sal has with his store, that's what needs to be fixed."

"Make it pretty so he wants to be there?" My heart drops to the pit of my stomach when her face scrunches into a frown full of pity and apprehension.

"What's wrong?" Sera takes a seat, staring between us. Her amber eyes creasing with concern. She still feels like a long-lost friend, as though we share something profound and unique, which is bizarre. We met yesterday.

"Ginny thinks we need to make the shop pretty so Sal wants to spend time in it," Paige says, swallowing hard.

"Oh." A thousand and one thoughts fly across their faces in a silent conversation that I'm not a part of.

"Then what is it?" I break in, desperate to stop my mood from deteriorating any further.

"We're limited to what we can say because we cannot interfere with your journey with your store, but we can explain about Sal's," Paige says, nodding to Sera.

"Yeah, we can do that." They sit closer and straighter, and I brace myself. "Storekeepers on the island are different from everywhere…"

"Nope." Paige shakes her head resolutely. "We cannot tell you that."

"Can we explain about the symbiotic relationship between house, store, and storekeeper?" Sera asks Paige, tapping her chin with her finger, her face creased to mock being deep in thought.

"No, but we can give her Sal's address so she could visit his house. Sal probably won't answer the door, but as Ginny is charged with caring for the store, and, therefore, the house, she can enter."

"Isn't that breaking and entering, or at least trespass?" I say quickly, fully expecting them to come to their senses.

"You can do anything connected to that store," Sera over-emphasizes each word. It sounds like there should be sound effects of at least a clap of thunder in the background.

"But that's the store, not the house." I rub my temple as my gran's statement about the house looking after you if you look after the store reverberates through my mind. Time to take the bull by the horns and voice what I really don't want to. "Piecing bits together from mainly what my gran has said. The house and store are magically linked to the storekeeper."

"If that's what your gran has more or less told you." Paige's bright, expectant eyes urge me on.

"If the storekeeper runs the store well, the house will care for and protect them." They give small nods. "If the storekeeper doesn't or can't, then the house... what?"

"Falls into disrepair and, the storekeeper, obscurity." A third woman wearing a short, leather jacket over an electric blue, leather bustier, with multiple facial piercings adds. "Hi, I'm Harley, another store holder. I popped into the bookstore, and Dray sent me over."

"Please tell me he sold you several books first. I need to clear some stock." Paige all but pleads.

"I'll get some later." Harley grimaces, looking away quickly.

"You returned some, didn't you?" Paige accuses, her head falling back.

"Sorry," Harley shrugs at Paige and turns to me. "I know you are worried the house will take offense at how crowded the store is and react."

"I can take some books." I offer, hoping that's what Harley is hinting at.

"She needs to clear about a thousand," Harley states, her jeweled nose ring glinting in the dim light. I adore the obvious friendship and unity these women share, despite how different they are. From biker chic Harley, to relaxed but trendy Paige, and, finally, just a tad too buttoned up Sera.

"And the rest." Sera snorts.

"Hey, it isn't that many." Paige waves her finger at them. "Is it?"

"That's a lot of books to sell. Are there even that many people on the island?" I get a pained look from them that matches the pressure building in my temple. "Don't tell me people don't actually buy stuff in the shops?"

"Most of it, you do, but my store acts as a second library as well. Loads of books are borrowed and returned."

"Can't the first library be extended?"

"No!" They all declare in unison, resolutely shaking their heads. I guess that told me.

"What is needed for Sal's store?" I decide to bring the conversation back to the topic at hand before I sip any more of the dry, crisp wine Draven ordered for us.

"You'll need to find something for him to sell. Which has to be something he has an affinity with. You'll need to help the store to welcome him back and accept the new goods." Sera explains.

"How?" I fumble the word, too lost to speak properly. My life is turning into a nightmarish fairytale.

They break into conversation, all talking over each other and throwing ideas around. Not even a tray of food being delivered stops them. The server takes in their animation and mouths *from Draven* with a wink. I sit back, pick up a tuna mayo roll and eat, waiting for them to reach some sort of consensus. When it goes on for a while, I munch on the fries.

Eventually, they stop yammering more because they need a drink than anything else.

"Well?"

"We have no idea." Sera gulps her wine. "Try Lillie The All-knowing."

"Is that an official title?" I really hope it is and that she's generous with it.

"No, and you'll need to get her talking. Good luck." Harley gives me a toothy grin that is not the least bit encouraging.

"How do I find Lillie The All-knowing?"

"Town Hall reception, if that fails, book an appointment with Hector and ask him how he anticipates you'll succeed." Sera squeezes my shoulder. "We'll help."

"Somehow." Harley grimaces.

"What can you tell me about Sal, then?" Friends, I fear in the days to come, this is the point I'll think back to and realize I should have vanished.

We eventually call it quits around six, and I decide to get my first look at Sal's store.

I learned a lot during the afternoon's fun Paige. adores books, believing each one is special, even if for no other reason than as an example of what a writer or editor shouldn't do. Her store is meant to sell new books, but every time the library gets a delivery, she takes the old ones they clear out.

As Whispering gets a copy of every book that any essence person had a part in producing, it's a lot. I can't help but feel she needs two distinct spaces.

Sera runs a clothing store, where most items are made by her family. That's how most of the stores are stocked. They become heirlooms and legacies bound together. Harley, a tattoo artist and piercer, is different. She took a unit over after arriving on the island a few years ago.

Sal's store is on the same side as the Emporium, but closer to the beach side of the island. I sense the despairing darkness shrouding it with choking hopelessness before I see the shadows concealing its desolate attempt to hide.

The exterior is made up of two massive display windows and a generous door, which appear in a good state of repair, but I can't see inside.

I twist the handle, and the door falls open. I step inside, ignoring the dense feeling of rejection.

The lights flicker to life, revealing dust and cobwebs, but little else. Bizarrely, I can tell the store is full of saleable works of art, even if they are not visible. Grimy glass counters that should display jewelry or other valuable small items are a void of neglect. The stands dotted around are wasting away under the pressure of isolation.

I wander further back, searching for some spark of life or clue as to what I need to do. My new friends told me Sal married into the family who kept the store, and they had made the treasures it has sold for centuries. However, each generation became more obsessed with their craft until none spared the time to have children. This is a heartbreaking story they seem to feel deep in their hearts because straight after that, they launched into a conversation about life away from their stores. Then insisted I join their book club. I was happy to agree.

My sanity and nearly my entire life have taught me shops do not have emotions. They cannot feel things, but as I wipe a line of dust coating a shelf, the store shudders like someone at the end of all they can endure receiving that much-needed hug that promises it will be okay.

When everyone is here on Sunday, we'll get it gleaming and fill it with life.

Tomorrow, I'll track down Sal and talk to him about his future plans. I presume people can sell the businesses, which might be his best option, as I think that, the lights turn off and a cold wind blows me outside.

The door resolutely clicks shut, and I face the prospect that this shop may not appreciate or even tolerate that idea.

Six

I had intended to wait until tomorrow to see the Emporium, but the urge to go now sings through me, lifting the lingering gloom of Sal's store.

Excited anticipation bubbles around me as I contemplate what my store sells. I have never asked, and no one has said. As I approach, my heart swells in my chest, and my eyes lock steadfastly on the protruding, glossy sign saying *Merchant's Emporium* in fancy silver calligraphy, with swirly black shadows painted on a gold background.

The last few momentous steps come with a burst of knowledge and visions that I'm too keyed up to consider.

I'm cautiously greeted with triple-glazed, white Georgian-style windows, which look like wooden frames but feel like metal. The tiny glass panels are nearly impossible to see through, thanks to a pattern on the middle sheet of glass. The robust, dark wood door has several peep holes, but the lack of windows gives an enter-at-peril air adding to the charm.

I run my hand over the solid brass, fist-shaped handle, ignoring the flare of searing heat shooting up my arm. It soon fades to a glowing warmth, and the lock snicks open. I venture inside and gasp for breath as shards of speculative scrutiny intrude my mind and heart, exploring my history and intentions.

A sudden blinding light threatens to expel me, but I stand my ground, urging the store to view me as a friend, an ally. As quick as it appeared, the light vanishes, leaving the store basked in darkness and shadows.

I ignore the resistance to my presence and push my way further inside, marveling at how normal this bizarre situation seems.

My eyes are gifted treasures to behold of every description and slowly roam the space with no idea what to rest on. It has everything, from fine jewelry to swords, books, ornate wooden and metal chests, and items of clothing. All ranging from new and possibly ancient. My store has an eclectic mix of merchandise.

A glass counter running down the left side houses most of the smaller objects. There's no obvious pattern or order as to how they're laid out, but I suspect every item is exactly where it needs to be. Most larger objects sit behind on overloaded, thick, well-used, wooden shelves.

A massive, mustard yellow sofa and two navy blue chairs, with a generous polished oak coffee table, take up the majority of the floor space.

The other side of the store is dominated by a majestic, black, steel cabinet set into a deep recess. It should fade into the background by rights but stands out with a dark, ominous alarm. I take several steps toward it, each becoming more difficult, like wading through treacle mixed with super glue. Seeking respite from the increased trembling in my legs, I sit on the nearest chair, expelling a long breath.

The cushioned, comfy seat engulfs me in a fragmented sense of command and being capable. I probe deeper into the living part of the Emporium. Wispy tendrils of hesitant welcome blend with uncertainty and loneliness. I yearn to reassure the store, but I'm unsure how or even if I should.

I scrunch my eyes to truly see the cabinet, and, slowly, a hazy, murky barrier becomes visible, shielding the world from the horrors and distress it contains. Today is not the day for me to explore those curiosities.

As I stand to leave, I notice the deep, burgeoned shelves on the back wall crammed full of strange, elongated teapots in every design and material imaginable. Genie lamps, thousands of them. Each fitting a genie somewhere in the world.

They call to me like a siren, and like the abandoned mortal I am, I yield to their allure and concede to my fate. Their aspiration for me encircles me, filling my empty heart with belonging, offering a future of kinship as I conform to their will.

I yank my hand back as a stinging pain slams across the back of it, reminding me of when my mother would slap my hand when I was a kid and reached for anything in a shop. I rub the tender red mark, summoning the courage to discover what hit me. The store is empty. I'm alone. There's no one here.

The lamps beckon me closer, and I admire their beauty, doing my best to convince myself my stinging hand is nothing more than my imagination.

"I have to strongly suggest you stay back from those," Gran says from the door, her unyielding presence gives me a boost of clarity and I heave in a much needed breath.

"Why? Gran, what slapped me?" The stammer in my voice draws her narrowed eyes to me.

"The store was protecting you." She comes to stand beside me, scanning my face.

"What from? They're so charming, even the ugly ones." Honestly, a few of them are quite grotesque, but their charm is not based on their exterior.

"That, my dear, is a story for another day." She stares wistfully. I can't help but follow her eye line to an elegant, silver genie lamp with lovingly crafted embossing on the base, top and delicate handle. It glows brightly, begging me to cherish it. Unable to stop myself, I reach for it. Gran's hand closes over my arm, holding it firm. "That is the last thing you should ever touch."

"But I have to!"

"The consequences are very severe." Her stern finality gives me the shove to drop my arm, and Gran relaxes beside me.

"What are the consequences?" I turn to her and find that, like mine, Gran's face is very expressive. All I see is honesty and a hint of fear.

"I wish, and I rarely use that word for obvious reasons, I could tell you."

"Then how do you know?" If I can't treasure my lamp, I want to understand why and what needs to change so I can.

"The same way I know I can't hold this one." She points to a stunningly ornate lamp with a fluted spout and bejeweled handle. The sheer level of detail gives it an air of ostentation that hinges on unappealing. "And your sister must never go near that one." Gran indicates another that brings a small, compassionate smile to my lips. It's by far the most stunning until you look closely. Because once you do, you see the myriad of imperfections that litter it. The microscopic holes where the inscription went too deep. The precious stones are not set precisely in the center of their engraved surrounding. It is both the best and worst.

It is in almost every way Rose. She's always on any list of the most beautiful or sexiest women, but her poor decisions have wrecked her life time and time again.

An urgent demand to protect Rose from her lamp and shelter it from her courses through me with an avalanche of protectiveness I haven't experienced for her since she was thirteen. That was when I realized she was almost compelled to choose the most disastrous option, regardless of the advice she received or from whom.

I stifle a yawn as fatigue crawls through my system.

"It's getting late. Have you had dinner?" I nod because we ate as we drank and laughed in the bar. "Then it's time to get some rest and come back when you're refreshed."

Gran herds me outside, and we walk around the side of my store.

"I didn't realize my house backed onto the Emporium." I muse. "Is there a way to get through without going around?"

"It has always seemed like there should be." Gran shrugs, but I hear her undertone of annoyance and something I can't place. We say our goodbyes, and I fall asleep as soon as my head hits the pillow.

The new day comes with a surge of energy, and unlike when I was in my twenties, it won't last forever, so I throw on shorts and a t-shirt and head for the Emporium.

Today's plan is to make my shop sparkle, then track down Gran to find out what is expected of me. After, I'll talk to Lillie The All-knowing and beg for any scrap of information about Sal's store and what I can do. On the periphery of what I want to accomplish is meeting Sal.

Loaded with cleaning supplies and breakfast pastries, my store opens the door as I approach. I put everything on the counter and survey it all in the bright light of day. I'd love to know what I thought would be different because nothing has changed.

I throw on my favorite high energy dance music playlist and twist my lips, deciding where to start. Some items, such as the old books and tapestries, will need specialized care. I'll check with Gran on who Aunt Valeria used.

I drag the rolling ladder to the end and climb with my supplies carefully tucked under my arm. It's far sturdier than the dainty wood would have me believe. Each shelf reveals a wealth of stock squeezed behind what can be seen from the ground. I bring them forward, then move the larger items to the back. How anyone is meant to purchase stuff they can't see is a mystery.

I make good progress and have everything I can reach from the ladder gleaming and sparkling within an hour. The sweltering temperature will make it harder, and I haven't seen anything that hints at air conditioning. My hands are baking in my gloves. I reach the ground and use it as an excuse to down a bottle of water, which is already tepid, despite spending the night in my fridge.

Needing to wash my sticky hands, I head through the door at the back, finding one of those high-tech fans that chill the air rather than merely blowing it around. I take several moments to luxuriate in the coolness.

The kitchenette is stocked with an enormous supply of coffees, creamers, and syrups. Everything from run-of-the-mill vanilla to a peppermint and bacon blend, which I move to the back.

A callosal fridge freezer takes up a good portion of the space. I open it with my fingers crossed to be rewarded with a dizzying array of cold drinks. I pull out an orange juice and press the icy bottle against the back of my neck. Apart from a few dubious ice cubes, the freezer is empty. Although it is gloriously big enough to climb inside when it gets even hotter later.

The room holds a few cabinets full of mugs and glasses. One for plates and cutlery. A closet for cleaning stuff. Squished against the wall, the table and chairs have a never-used atmosphere about them.

I slide the ladder along, secure it, and head back up. By the time the next section is done, so am I, at least for a while. I'm sweaty, grimy, and probably bright red. Heat is not really a friend of mine, no matter how much I covet it.

A quick shower and fresh clothing later, I feel like a new woman, ready to ask Gran the tough questions. I borrow a scooter and decide to tackle Lillie The All-knowing first.

The town hall is exactly the same on the outside, but, inside, it resembles a barn. My pastel, floral mini-dress and strappy sandals become a plaid shirt, jeans, and cowboy boots, complete with spurs.

"He could at least make it something real people wear." A gentleman who had been wearing a toga huffs loudly, shaking his head at his new attire. I stifle my chuckle and make a beeline for the counter. When Sera mentioned her name, I instinctively knew she was talking about the purple haired, efficient, and untalkative receptionist who gave me my card at the Town Hall.

"Hi, Lillie, I was hoping you could assist me with some information about how to help Sal's store over a cold drink."

"Here or in the big wide world?" There's an edge to her question and sadness hidden in her silver, triangular eyes.

"Ideally, both." I grin, holding two ice-cold sodas for her to pick. She takes one, grabs a file, and indicates for me to follow her to a small table half-shielded from the main reception. I pull a notepad and pen from my bag. "Bearing in mind, I know nothing about the island, stores, or people, or the relationship between them. What can you tell me?"

"In what capacity are you asking?" Her very formalized question stops me as I gulp a mouthful of sparkling, fruit flavored water.

"What are my choices?"

"You are responsible for the Merchant's trading center, also known as the Emporium, which is currently without a registered Merchant, so that is an option. You have been tasked with the recuperations of Sal's store, so that is a second. You are new to the island and the essence world. That's another two." Lillie tilts her head, eyebrows slightly raised, waiting for my response.

"Could I ask in all those ways?"

"Yes." I wait for a beat. She says nothing more.

"Then I am asking in all those ways."

"I'm summing this up, so you may have further questions. The stores are the lifeblood of the island, its purpose and energy. If anything happens to damage a store, it affects the kismet that keeps Whispering running."

"I thought the kismet was the same for all essence people? Does the island have its own supply?" My foggy understanding leaves even more to be desired than I anticipated.

"Yes, and no. It is all the same kismet, and it runs through everything and everyone essence. From people whose essence is so diluted it is no longer discernible, all the way to the eminence himself. It fuels what is needed; however that is. Whispering is unique, so what it does here is different from anywhere else." Lillie casts a quick gaze around. "How the kismet actually does what it does is a mystery. Many have speculated, but no one truly knows the full truth. It just is."

"That is not helpful." I don't mean to grumble, but that was as clear as mud.

"Did you expect a scientific, analytical explanation for actual magic?" She cocks her head, lighter shades of pink merrily cascading through her long purple hair. It's spectacular, but possibly her way of laughing.

"Only a little bit." I chuckle. I was fully anticipating precisely that.

"Sorry to disappoint." Lillie grows thoughtful. "You'll learn more about the kismet and essence over time. If you stay with the Emporium, it should provide you with the information you need and when. Otherwise, it might burst into your mind in one fell swoop, which is not always pleasant."

"I've had a taste of that. It was okay, but it has not been more than factoids, really." The snippets that come to me do not amount to much of anything. "What about Sal?"

"Sal's store has been in his late wife's family since one of her ancestors conjured it from nothing. Since then, they have created all the items it has ever stocked or sold and only they supplied the staff. The relationship between the store and the family grew more extraordinarily obsessive each year. It is the most extreme Whispering has known. The connection was unbreakable and zealous. When they died out, the store lost its purpose. Many believe it fell into a profound sense of mourning that it may not recover. The detrimental changes to Sal suggest he inherited the connection from his wife's family."

Lillie shows me photographs of different people standing in front of the store. As the generations progress, their creepy attachment deepens until the edges of the people blend with the store. I could not tell you where one ends and the other begins.

"This was taken when Sal moved to Whispering and took over running the store." Lillie lays down a similar image, where Sal stands out like someone colorized him in a black-and-white photo.

"Oh." I admire Sal's pride, but his total lack of awareness is disheartening.

"And this was days before his wife died." I brace myself as Lillie places another photograph in front of me.

Sal is standing outside the store, his arms resolutely crossed over his chest as he guards it. Devoid of color, expression, and even a good foot shorter, he's a shadow of the man he was. The queasiness in my stomach combines unpleasantly with the swirling.

"It's a lot to take in," Lillie tells me compassionately. "Most believe the store can be saved."

"Do I need to find products or a purpose?" The confusion bubbling around my mind trips into my words, but just as I get to grips with it, I think of something else she said. "They conjured the store? Not built it?"

"The family were witches, looking for somewhere to display their art, potions and whatever else they could concoct. Back then, witches had no part in manual labor, not on Whispering, anyway." Lillie leans forward and stares intently at me. I swallow and make notes, eager for a reason to look away. "With that store, purpose and products are likely the same."

"Display? Not sell?" Her sympathetic frown confirms that I sound like a bewildered parrot.

"They were not worried about exchanging it for money. That was the only way to clear space for new items."

I decide to leave the historical aspect of the conversation behind or I'll be here for the rest of the day and get nowhere. "Isn't there anyone who could have helped Sal or the store sooner?"

Lillie gives me an assessing stare, and I have no idea what she's searching for or if she finds it. "The Merchant."

"My aunt."

"Was the Merchant, but the role has been vacant for a while."

"How long?" I demand because anger seeps through me like a sharp knife I can't stop.

"Long enough." Lillie deflates, and her gaze darts around. "Look, I cannot explain why or how, but matters outside our control changed and shit over the islanders and their establishments."

"How come you get to swear here, and I don't?" Not the most important or relevant question, but her pained expression promises she can't give me the information I really want.

"I don't usually, but more is being discovered and..." She trails off, watching Hector flounce past us and outside. "Whispering Isle needs as much help as it can get." Lillie closes her mouth to a firm line.

"Fancy lunch?" I need to discover what she's practically biting her tongue to stop from spilling out.

"I can't do lunch." Her shoulders drop as she stands, ending our conversation.

"I presume you know which house is mine. Pop over anytime." I write my number on a piece of paper and hand it over. "Call me. I'm always open to making new friends."

"Thanks." I leave her staring at the piece of paper. Caught between wanting to drag every last morsel of information from her and not liking how suspiciously she looked at me.

Seven

My next port of call is Gran, and I eventually find her in the first place I should have looked, her house. Her dark red brick, three-story townhouse sits uncomfortably among rows of whimsical cottages. The carefree, untroubled atmosphere granted by the pastel exteriors and flower-filled gardens stumbles when I open Gran's gate and walk into her paved courtyard.

Her black, wrought-iron front door lacks the warmth the porches provide in every other property around us. The white doorbell has a camera, and I press a button, suspecting she's alerted the second anyone steps across her boundary.

The door opens, and Jerry stands to the side, inviting me in. The interior is no less austere, and her sitting room reminds me of a period TV drama. Leather-bound books and strange ornaments that don't resemble anything fill the dark wood built-ins lining the walls.

The urge to stand until someone tells me I can sit is hard to resist, but I do as I'm visiting a relative and not being called to the principal's office. Although the overly firm, dark green leather chair makes standing the best option.

"Ginny, how lovely to see you. Jerry is preparing some refreshments." Gran gracefully lowers herself opposite me. "I was about to come and find you."

"Oh, what for?" I blame my sudden burst of misgiving on how much her house reminds me of Lawrence's dream home.

"Lunch, then maybe sight-seeing or shopping." Jerry brings in a tray with a pitcher of lemonade, glasses with ice, and a plate of cookies, places it on the small table between Gran and me, winks at her, and leaves. I pretend not to notice how heated their exchange is or how she's staring at his backside. Go, Gran.

"I need to talk to you about the store and the Merchant."

"I had a feeling." Gran pours drinks and hands me a cookie. "If it's ever relevant, you'll know everything you need about both."

"Gran, that doesn't help." I sigh.

"One day, this will either be a slightly strange but very faded memory or a profound defining and seminal life moment. There's no in between. It will be all or nothing. My grandmotherly advice is to follow the path you are on to the best of your abilities and be watchful. If it's meant to be, it will be."

"And if it's not?" In the back of my mind, the niggling thought of asking what it is yammers away at me, unheeded.

"You always have a home." Her hand covers mine. "There are so many roles and jobs on Whispering; you'll find something you love. You are a planner; for a while, just let the future happen."

My heart rate speeds, and my chest constricts. Having a plan is comforting, and targets give me something to aim for. How will I know if I've claimed my new life if I don't know what it looks like?

The futility of that hits me square in the stomach. I deliberately chose an unknown place because it was different from what I had. An adventure, those should not come with a cozy itinerary.

"Can I have more grandmotherly advice on how to help Sal and his store?"

"They both need a future. Something to help them move on." She sits back, sipping her iced lemonade. My lips curl upwards because she does the same little scowl as the twins when they're stuck on a problem. "I wish I knew what it was, but I don't."

"Is there something?" Her eyes dart to mine, full of apprehension.

"I believe so." She says carefully, biting her lower lip. "But I cannot be certain."

"What happens to them if there isn't?" Dread curls around me as Gran's trembling hand makes the glass clatter on the tray as she puts it down.

"The store could fade to nothing. Leaving either a blank shell of apathy that may spread through the row or disappear altogether. Same for Sal."

"It could be infectious?" The stores on each side were vibrant and full of life. The one selling musical instruments was teeming with song and dance. The other was full of giggling children exploring the toys.

Gran says nothing, which is the answer I didn't want.

"Is there any chance it could be good for both of them?" I try to bat away the confusion and hopelessness clouding my good intentions because all I have so far are warnings and no clue how to help.

"There is always a chance." Gran hides her wince by taking a bite of a cookie.

"Gran, has anything changed on the island recently?"

"Such as?" Gran's spine straightens to ramrod straight, and her tone snaps to pure power.

"Anything." I mumble, amazed and shaken by the sudden transformation of the woman who supplied me with just about all the childhood love I ever received.

"Do not concern yourself with such matters." She softens, and for a fleeting moment, she's the gran I knew as a child.

"I need to talk to Sal. Any idea how?" With the air growing increasingly inhospitable, I'm ready to be somewhere else.

"Go to his house and say what you need to. If you're going to get any joy, it will be there. Do you want me to come?"

"Thanks, but it feels like something I should do alone." I cast Gran a quick look and see her little nod. "Gran, have I bitten off more than I can chew?"

"Probably not." She shakes her head, her face creasing into the smile I love, the one that is warm and affectionate. Reserved for special moments. "But it may be more than you want, and that is fine."

We spend a while chatting about anything and everything, but nothing important. I'm not even invited to see the rest of her home. I ride the scooter away, convinced there's far more going on than I can imagine.

※ ※ ※ ※

Sal's house is the near derelict colonial property cocooned in deathly obscurity I found on my way to watch the sunrise. The shadows banishing the light and shrouding it in darkness are made all the more eery by the bright sun and high temperature.

I push up the path, fearing that a hand will shoot from a bush and drag me into a burning inferno of ghosts, ghouls, and other stuff I refuse to name. The front door flies wide open, and my mouth rounds in a silent scream.

"Sal, are you home?" I call, willing my heart rate to slow, and cheering myself for making it inside while trying not to gag on the musty smell. "I brought food. Pizza."

It was Gran's parting suggestion. I place the box on the grubby table, open it, and take a slice. A figure that could be anything humanoid peers around a door.

"Wow, this pizza is good. Why has no one told me?" That is not only helpful, but the absolute honest truth. It's out of this world delicious. "Quick, or I might scarf the lot."

He skulks in, and I get a proper glimpse of him. Graying skin, frayed hair, ragged clothing hanging from a bunched-up, boney body. He makes the final photograph Lillie showed me look positively glowing with health and vitality.

"Sit with me, please." I break off a slice and hand it out. Sal warily steps further into the room, his nose twitching as he takes it. Just when I think he's going to bolt, he moves the chair several feet from the table and hovers over it, almost sitting. I give him my friendliest grin. "Thanks."

"Why are you here?" His voice is gravelly as if he hasn't spoken for a long time.

"I came to the island because my husband got another, much younger, woman pregnant, and I wanted a new future to claim as my own. Then, collecting my card in the town hall, I swore." He croaks in what I think is a laugh. I give an exaggerated and playful shrug. "My correction was to help a store. I chose yours. Please, help me."

I'm banking on him having that me-man-me-fix stake that rolls through most men.

I munch a second slice and push the box over as Sal hunches further in on himself, ready to dart away.

"This is all new to me. Buildings don't have emotions where I'm from. They are built, not conjured. I am more than a little lost." I don't need to put in any effort to make my voice sound small and bleak. I just stop faking anything else.

"It takes a leap of trust." He ambles, almost hugging the pizza.

"Trust has always been an issue for me, and, recently, my ability took a battering." I swallow to soothe my parched throat, pull two drinks from my bag, and pass one over.

"I remember it was hard, but I had my Ida. She made it... worthwhile." I witness his grief flicker through him and into the house. "She was the store."

I let him dwell for a few moments.

"Sal, do you mind if I open the door? I'm not acclimatized to this heat. Where I used to live, it was usually raining." He shakes his head, but his eyes widen in alarm. I slide the double patio doors open, which doesn't give much relief but does alleviate the musty air.

"Ida loved the yard. It was her place away from the studio."

"I'm sorry for your loss. Saying goodbye is the hardest." I let him finish his slice before adding. "Isn't it?"

He nods with no conviction.

"How can we help the store to do that?" Waiting for his response is agony. "I've been told it needs a new purpose. Do you think that is a good strategy?"

He stays quiet for an eternity as he debates this, but, eventually, his complexion improves marginally. "Yes."

"That's a relief because I had nothing else." I put my hand on my chest, playing up the damsel in distress angle. "I'm hoping helping your store will benefit me in understanding my aunt's needs from me as well."

"Both the store and I will be honored to assist." His expression grows worryingly somber. "That is the store that leads. If there's anything we can do, please tell us."

"Could we get together and see what ideas we can come up with? Maybe with other store holders?"

"I can't think of any reason why not." How tense he's grown and how wide his eyes are, show just how damned hard he fought to find one.

"My place tonight, say, about seven. I'll go round up the troops and sort some food; any preferences?"

Sal shakes his head, fading in on himself.

"I really do appreciate your help. I hate to disappoint my gran, and I'd hate to tell Oompa I failed. Damn, please don't tell Hector or anyone I call him that."

Sal gives a rusty chuckle. "You have my word."

"Phew, see you in a few hours." I exit swiftly, leaving him the remaining pizza, not only because he desperately needs sustenance but in the hopes it will remind him of the good things. I haven't left my number, so he won't be able to contact me to cancel, and I suspect he's too much of a gentleman to stand me up.

I text Harley, Paige, and Sera. They all message back within moments, agreeing to come. Harley sets up a group chat, which is more about debating food and wine than helpful suggestions. I couldn't love it more, though. A quick stop off at the town hall, I've roped a dazed Lillie in, and I lose no time adding her to the chat.

When there's still no consensus on wine or food after a thirty-minute debate, that isn't helped by Lillie commenting that everything sounds good. I buy twelve different bottles of wine, order pizza, because it really was great pizza, and a Mexican platter.

Eight

Hosting people for the first time as a single woman, and since coming to Whispering, is daunting. I console myself that I don't need to fret about Lawrence getting bored and, therefore, rude. He is insufferable when he's not being adequately entertained or the center of attention.

I pace the length of the house again and wander into the back garden. It's bigger than I expected. The lawn is surrounded by opulent flower beds, swarming with tropical plants, giving off a tranquil floral scent that's very addictive. A large patio sits under a shady pergola, with vines growing up the sides. For a moment, I debate moving us outside to enjoy the evening air but decide I cherish the air conditioning more.

My fingers twitch to dig out the weeds, also calling this plot of land home, but as I don't know what should be there and what shouldn't, I would probably remove some locally prized flowers.

The knock at the door startles me, and I swallow my nerves as I head to answer it.

Paige waltzes in, carrying a bottle of wine. Her short sleeve, French navy jumpsuit is the perfect blend of smart casual and the belted waist shows off her slim figure. Followed by Sera, who brings yet more wine. Then Lillie, who hesitates until I nearly yank her inside.

"I bought beer." Lillie twists around, holding up a six-pack. "Is beer okay?"

"You didn't need to bring anything, but beer sounds great. Glass?" I stare at the kitchen cabinets, wondering which one holds the glasses, and open the one that glows, thanking the house for helping me. Then gulp a large glass of sparkling white wine because I now live in a world where the houses and shops are alive, and the town hall changes daily. Oh, and did I mention people shift to and from large animals on the street? I nearly fell off the scooter this afternoon when a four-foot-nothing bloke became a behemoth polar bear.

One moment, he was a man, then he was a polar bear. A big, scary polar bear, with thick fur, who instantly bounded in my direction. I was too shocked to move, but his actual bear hug more than made up for it.

I give Lillie her glass and accept the beer she offers. If I keep downing wine, I'll be as drunk as a skunk within an hour.

"Harley will be a bit late. She had a last-minute piercing appointment. My kids are with their dad, so I'm not leaving early," Paige announces, taking a seat and almost inhaling her large glass of wine.

"Do they see him often?" I ask, plonking my backside in the chair nearest the door.

"He and his wife are doing their house up as a tenth wedding anniversary gift, so not as much, but, usually, it's a few nights during the week and every other weekend. It's been the same since..." She's cut off by the thudding door, and we fall into an eager silence.

Sal is welcomed by a barrage of enthusiastic greetings that do nothing to soothe his tense frame or gaunt expression. As I anticipated he hasn't showered but has changed his shirt, albeit to one not much better than he was wearing earlier. Given apprehension overshadowing him, he did well to get here.

"Paige was telling us about how her baby daddy is doing his house up and doesn't see the children as much at the moment." I tell Sal, holding up wine and beer for him to pick. He chooses beer and declines a glass. I retake my seat, giving him no option but to join us.

The slow realization of what Paige's words mean pierces my mind with the subtlety of a bull in a China shop.

"Did you say tenth wedding anniversary? He was married when both kids were conceived?" I try, and I mean really hard, not to let my betrayal by Lawrence alter how I feel about this, but it's tough. I have to lower my hands to avoid anyone seeing them tremble.

The women look anywhere but at me. The atmosphere has gone from jovial to awkward to frankly mortifying in a heartbeat.

"It's a shifter thing." Sal gently explains. "Paige and Arne are shifters, his wife isn't, and I don't mean to speak ill of her because my Ida was the same, but she isn't very understanding of the full moon."

"Oh, okay." I gulp my drink, and I really should swap to soda or a good strong whisky.

"You have no idea what I mean by the full moon, do you?" Sal asks, and I applaud his grit because his wringing hands and hovering on the seat reveal his anxiety. I shake my head.

"Shifters have a hormone surge at the full moon that calls them to mate. It's overwhelming, inconvenient, and beyond our control." He tells me sadly. Paige nods, her head dipped. "Most shifters attend a Throng. There are a few regular ones on the island each month. Think of them as sort of like an orgy or a sex club. But some people have arrangements with friends to help each other."

Orgy, sex clubs? Each month? For uncontrollable hormone surges? I'm not sure what to make of that.

A GENIE'S NEW START

"Arne and I were friends and started at the same time. Neither of us wanted to go to a Throng, so we didn't." The words rush from Paige in a miserable tumble as her eyes plead for understanding. "We were going to stop when he mated Tiffany, but their first full moon together was a disaster. It nearly destroyed their relationship. The next day, she begged me to restart the arrangement. I agreed." Her voice falls to a pained whisper. "She was such a mess, I couldn't not."

"Well, good." I get several skeptical looks and sighs. "I'm not going to pretend to understand, but if you all agree, and she knows, it's different. My soon to be ex-husband got another woman pregnant. I found out when she arrived at my door begging me to let him go because they were in love." My skin burns with humiliation. I rub my forehead and take solace from Sera and Lillie supportively rubbing my arms. "She was barely older than our children."

"Sounds like you're better off without him." Paige's upper lip curls up as she growls menacingly.

"Yes, I am." I agree.

"My situation is very different. Tiffany is an imp, they have issues getting pregnant, especially with a shifter mate, and it was her suggestion that we have a baby. We all co-parent, and it works great."

"Wow, that's fantastic." I reach over and squeeze her hand. "Honestly, if it works for you, it really is."

"I let myself in, hope that's okay. What did I miss?" Harley, clad in skin tight, darkest green, leather pants and a matching jacket, opens one of the beers she bought and puts the rest in my fridge. I never would have thought I'd love the whole, your home, my home thing, but I do.

"We just shocked the pants off Ginny by telling her my baby daddy is married." Paige's overly cheerful words make me feel bad for judging her.

"Yeah, that'll do it. You shifters are a rowdy bunch." She jokes, pulling a comical face, and just like that, we're all back to as we were.

"Excuse me, miss high and mighty, but I seem to recall that you have shifter blood." Paige accuses, waving her finger, doing her best to maintain her scowl and not laugh.

"Yep, but I'm blessed to rarely be affected by the full moon." Harley dramatically shakes her head and throws her long black hair over her shoulder in a jokey one-up-on-you way before poking her tongue out at Paige.

"Not that rare. You succumb to the dark side often enough to be classed as rowdy." Sera sits up, deliberately looking down her nose at Harley. "Unlike pure-as-the-driven-snow me."

"Snow that's driven on is anything but pure." I point out before my eyes widen, and my mouth hangs open in shock at my own words. Everyone bursts out laughing, even Lillie and Sal.

I leave them to their banter when the food delivery guy walks up the front path. The smell of gooey cheese and spicy chicken halts the conversation better than anything I could have tried.

Within seconds, literally seconds, I barely saw them move, they all have food.

"I'm going to put on too much weight if all the food is this good," I murmur around an aromatic chicken and rice burrito.

"There are no calories or fat in the food on Whispering," Lillie tells me earnestly.

"Really!" I take a larger bit, no longer worried about my waistline.

"No!" Harley laughs, high-fiving Lillie. "If anything, the opposite. Everything is made with butter and full-fat everything."

"That's gutting. I believed you. I was about to order cake." I want to pout and stamp my foot, or at least cry a little, but grin instead.

"Desserts don't," Lilly promises. I'm halfway to my phone before I come to my senses.

"You're evil." I point an accusing finger at her, now actually pouting. Her hair becomes a virtual light display in shades of pink and purple.

"Helping a store overcome loss is arduous work." Sal says, pulling his phone and frowning at the screen as he taps away. "It'll burn up calories."

I try not to examine him too closely because everyone is doing it openly, and I don't want him to feel any more on display than he already does. But the man within him emerges a bit more with each word.

"Talking about the store." I pick up my pen, open my notebook, and aim my questions at Sal. "It needs a purpose. Are there guidelines about what they can be? Do we ask it?"

"Nothing like guidelines or rules. How would it answer if we asked?" He cocks his head at me. "How would we ask?"

"Could we go there and make suggestions?" I offer.

"You could try. If it doesn't like the idea, I'm sure you'll know." Lillie twists her lips. "Maybe go with a list to give plenty of choices and narrow it down over a few tries."

"Right, let's brainstorm suggestions." I stare from one to the other, waiting for an idea, literally anything. I'm met with blank faces.

"How did you decide on your stores?"

"Mine has been in my family for a long time. It was always books." Paige shrugs.

"Same for mine." Sera sits back, sipping her wine thoughtfully.

"Mine was a haberdashery, but the holders wanted to retire, and there was no one to take it over. Besides, most people already purchased sewing supplies from Sera's store anyway. I asked it if it could swap to a tattoo and piercing parlor. It agreed." Harley says around a mouth of pizza. My busy mind files away her British use of haberdashery.

"Books. Apparently, according to Drey, I have too many." Paige's disbelieving tone earns snorts from Sera and Harley. "You two, too?"

"I was kind of scared they'd topple, and we'd be buried alive." I pipe up while writing books on my list of options. "What else?"

"Art. There's always someone artistic around looking to sell something." Harley adds.

Sera bolts forward, catching us all off guard. "There isn't a frozen yogurt place."

"And there won't be," Paige shudders. "Please, Sal, no frozen yogurt."

"I'll do my best." He nods.

"I thought the store had to agree?"

"The holder has some sway. Especially for anything they really do or don't want." Sal explains.

"Then, Sal, what do *you* want?" Lilly asks him, emphasizing the word you, forcing him to think about what he truly wants for his future.

"I've never thought about it." He swallows, and his complexion turns a bit more ashen.

"What interests you?" I try for a change of tack.

"Repairing stuff, but I was never very good. Too many leftover bits."

"Anything else? Just list stuff you like or enjoy, and we can work on it."

"Reading. My old motorbike. Cars. Making beer. Trying to figure out how things worked. Boats. Skiing. White water rafting. Scuba diving. Teaching."

"Reading could tie into the books. Would a brewery be possible?" I get several nods. "I haven't seen any cars or motorbikes, and I presume there isn't any skiing."

"There's the dry slop, but that's all. Would it need to be white water rafting? How about something like paddle-boarding or surfing? It would go well with scuba-diving." Sera's tone has gone very business-like, which is possibly her go-to setting. Even tonight, she's in a pencil skirt and a chignon blouse.

"That could work." Sal leans back in his chair, eyes wide, and while not clear, they are not as shielded.

"What did you teach?" I ask.

"Nothing. I was about to start training when I met Ida, but it never happened. I was trying to decide between English and History."

"See, books." Paige crosses her arms resolutely over her chest. "We can have you up and running by Monday."

We all ignore her.

"Would a learning resource center be possible?" I'm thinking way outside of the box, but nothing about this run-of-the-mill.

"Ohh, that could be fun." Sal's eagerness is a balm to my soul that I take as a personal win.

"It would be possible. You could have guest speakers and workshops." Lillie nods quickly. "The store would need some hefty renovations that it might not like, but it's a doable option."

After retiring to the garden when the dessert arrives, we spend the next few hours talking about who could teach what. Most of the names mean nothing to me, but that's fine. I'll meet more people over time. When they all leave at midnight, the house breathes out a sigh.

Nine

I wake up restless, and my feet twitch to get going. After a quick shower, I dress in pale green, mid-thigh shorts and a dark green t-shirt and head to the Emporium after a quick trip to the grocery store to stock up on ice lollies. They're to help me make the most of my time before I meet Sal at ten by his store. I'm protective of both of them and keeping fingers and toes crossed, that we find a resolution.

The Emporium welcomes me with a soft swirl of air that wraps me in unity, reminding me of the camaraderie of last night. Just before everyone finally left, we drunkenly toasted to our mutual stores and their continued prosperity.

I start cleaning and rearranging the next section. Falling in love with a set of porcelain thimbles that go from baby to huge man size, all hand painted with various mythical sea creatures. One of the larger ones is especially captivating, A woman with long, strawberry blonde hair, pretty blue eyes, and the most perfect, cherry red lips. The more I stare, mesmerized, the more real it appears. My gaze locks on the largest of a merman with a colorful tattoo depicting a coral reef and long dark hair pulled back. A shocked scream rips from my throat when he winks at me, and I have a scream that features in horror movies. My sister has copied it in more than one part.

"Ginny! I got you." I shriek louder as huge hands wrap around my waist, yanking me from the ladder.

My feet make contact with the ground, and I scramble back, falling into a defensive stance.

"It's only me." Draven quirks an amused eyebrow at me before scanning everything. "What were you screaming at?"

I stare from him to the shelf and back again. It's twelve feet in the air and on the other side of the counter.

"How?" I croak as my heart decides to start beating and races at an alarming pace.

"Sometimes my dragon will loan me his wings." Draven waves off my question before I can ask more. "Why did you scream?"

"The..." I close my mouth, not wanting to tell him a thimble winked at me because, honestly, who the hell would believe that? Draven closes the distance between us, standing inches away. His body heat seeps into me. If I leaned forward a smidgeon, I'd be pressed against him. I would no longer have to wonder what my cutie's muscles feel like.

Which is something I've spent far too many hours fantasizing about.

"You're safe. If there's anything evil, I will not let it harm you." His calloused hands run down my arms.

"The merman on the thimble winked at me." I blurt to stop my mind from taking my body on an X-rated sideshow. His gorgeously intense gray eyes crinkle, and his mouth curves upward.

"The thimble winked at you?" His attempts not to let his laughter into his voice fail.

"What, so your dragon can lend you wings? Shops can have emotions and food, no calories, but a merman on a thimble can't wink at me?" I thrust my hands on my hips and glare at him.

"I believe you." Draven holds his hands up in surrender. "But why did you scream like the terror was chasing you?"

"I can't believe I'm saying this again. The merman on the thimble winked at me. He's painted on a thimble." I pinch the bridge of my nose and sink onto the sofa. "Figures painted on things don't do that."

Draven folds himself into a chair, resting his elbows on his knees. "This store is full of items that do the unexpected. Nothing in here is completely normal. Usually, the more ordinary it looks, the more peculiar or powerful it is."

"Powerful?" I lean forward until my bottom is almost off the seat.

"As in magical," Draven says gently but firmly. "Did you say food with no calories?"

I do a double-take at his change of subject. His disbelievingly optimistic expression is comical and probably identical to mine last night.

"That was Lillie's joke on me. She said the food on Whispering had no fat or calories, and I fell for it because nothing else here follows the normal rules of what is possible." I huff because the one thing I would dearly love to be true never will be, and I ate enough last night for my waistline to expand several inches.

"Ahh. I'll make sure Percy is going to behave." Draven heads to the shelves, giving me a perfect eye line to the delectable contours of his firm behind.

"Wait, did you say Percy? The thimble has a name?" I stagger after Draven, catching his arm. His muscles ripple below my palm, and I let go before I start purring. He nods down at me. "How did Percy get in the thimble? Does he need to be released?"

"Percy isn't a real person."

"Of course, he's not. I knew that." Draven's brow hits his hairline. "Okay, I didn't know that, but how would I?"

"Percy was a real merman a long time ago. A witch trapped the essence of him and his family in the thimbles, making them ordinary, land-walking humans."

"That was horrible! Why would anyone do such a thing? How do I free him?" A sudden need to protect Percy settles in my core, churning through my swirling emotions that have been spun into an eddy already today.

"The witch was terminated before anyone found out how to free him or why she did it."

"There has to be a way. Families can't stay trapped forever. It just isn't right, Draven." My voice has risen several octaves, and I risk summoning all the dogs on Whispering.

"It was one of the things your aunt was working on before her wonderlust got too strong." Draven's calm patience soothes some of my anger for the mere family reduced to existing in tiny pieces of innate porcelain.

My alarm blasts a high-pitched wailing, and I swear the store groans.

"I need to meet Sal in a bit. Percy will have to wait a tad longer." I go into the small staff room and wash my hands when a random thought occurs to me. "What did you mean, the terror?"

"That's a conversation for another time, but if anything here or anywhere else has a particularly strong emotional or nounful signature, call me." Draven passes me a card with his number, email, and several bits of information printed on it. I slide it into my pocket.

"Nounful?"

"If it's ever relevant, you'll know what I mean." I let that go because my poor brain can only take so much in one day. Between finding out about Percy and having to ask a store if it can become a learning center, today's limit has been reached.

⚱ ⚱ ⚱ ⚱

I see Sal shuffling from foot to foot halfway between our stores. In the bright light of day, he looks more human, and the haze clouding his features has eased. He scrubs his hand through his hair, giving it a messy look that matches his creased shirt and trousers. They're different from the ones he had yesterday, that were none too fresh, and he smells of shower gel rather than trapped, humid air. It's all a step in the right direction.

"I'm really thirsty. Could we get a drink first?" I say, walking into a quaint, 1950s-style diner with pale blue gingham tablecloths and guitars hanging from the wall. "Is ten am too early for a banana split? It is fruit."

In my defense, part of me is in vacation mode, and the other part is too hot and sweaty to care. I also skipped breakfast.

"No, but the apple pie here is better." Sal sits hunched in on himself, trying to ignore the people staring.

"Then apple pie it is." I signal the waitress and order quickly. She stands just behind Sal, who looks intently at the table. Her face contorts with her battle not to spill the words of encouragement hovering on her tongue.

"How are we going to talk to the store?" I say as the waitress backs away.

"You're the Merchant; you just do." Sal exclaims, his head shooting up.

"I'm helping my aunt with the Emporium, I suppose that sort of makes me a merchant."

"No, you're *The* Merchant." Sal's features snap into sharp focus. I swallow the lump in my throat and raise my hand to my chest to stop my thundering heart beating clean out of it.

Eyes bore into me from every angle, and I struggle to catch my breath. The room spins as the term the Merchant drives around my skull like a damn race car in the Indie 500.

"I've spoken out of turn." Sal states, the shroud descending to conceal his whole face.

"No, I'm sure you didn't. But I haven't been called that before. It is strange, familiar and weird. I can't even describe it." My hands rotate from burning to icy in quick succession, and my gut twists painfully. And my inner swirl of emotions finds a new hell for leather gear. The urge to embrace the Merchant and reject it is equally compelling.

The waitress brings our drinks and pie. This time, I'm the one she fights not to empathize with. As we're both the object of people's fascination, we eat quickly and escape.

I link my arm through Sal's and almost drag him up the street. He stops dead, taking deep, faltering breaths a few steps from the border of his store.

"You got this."

"I haven't been here since..." He backs away. "My Ida loved it. Her whole family did. It was their thing. I was only there because of them."

"What does it mean to you?" His mouth opens and closes until he offers a dejected shrug. "Let's find out then."

Sal straightens his spine, adding several inches to his height. "If the store and I are not right for each other, then we must set the other free."

"Absolutely," I say with much more conviction than I can summon. I'm still reeling from being called the Merchant and still have no idea why.

I stay back as Sal approaches the door, casting a panicked look at me when it clicks open. I follow him in and wait.

The air is almost too stale and bleak to cope with, or it could be the total sense of loss cascading from every inch of the building. The actual appearance is far different from when I was here alone. The artwork is visible, and the racks are normal. I suspect I saw how it feels.

Sal wanders aimlessly around, running his hand over some of the items. Pausing to stare at other pieces. It's all stunning and unbelievably varied. I can see why the family needed somewhere to display it.

"Does the store understand they have all passed?"

"It understands that I am the last, but it is confused by what that means." Sal stands behind the counter, grabs a cloth, and dusts the ancient till.

"How do we explain it?"

"We reassure it there's a future. If not with my plan, then another will be found." The air thins and lightens, not by much but enough to notice.

"How is this for you?"

"I hadn't expected it to still feel like mine, but it does." He lifts a box on the counter and lays several drawings out. "We both need to clear this out before we can look to the future."

"A clearance sale?" I've always loved a bargain, but who doesn't?

"Of sorts." Sal agrees, moving on to retrieve further items. I quickly get caught up in the euphoria of gathering exquisite pieces of art that are meant to be mine. A painting for Rose, an ornate notepad for Ruby, and a wooden carving of a basketball game for Owen are among my many treasures.

Sal wraps and packs it all in a box, carefully labeling each item. When I'm done, I stand in the center, gleefully rubbing my hands.

"That's birthdays and Christmas sorted." I hold my credit card out and brace myself. "What's the damage?"

"Damage?"

"How much does it come to?"

"I could never charge the Merchant." Sal rigorously shakes his head.

"I am not the Merchant. Please tell me how much." The denial sits unhappily within me as irrefutable proof that I need to do some urgent research.

I take no notice as Sal pushes a number into the card reader, and I enter my pin.

"Purely for curiosity's sake, how would this be different if I was the Merchant?"

"Beats me, because if you are, you are." Sal cryptically waves off the question that took me an eternity to voice. "Have you got everything?"

I rummage around once more, and, as I'm about to tell him I have it all, I come across a silver tankard that's seen better days. It's been knocked and scuffed multiple times and has very little beauty left. Yet, despite that, or maybe because of it, it belongs in the Emporium. Protected while it waits to be claimed.

"Who on earth are you giving that to?" Sal scratches his head, scowling at the tankard.

"The Emporium." I wait for him to tell me to stop being silly and put it back because it has no worth, but he reverently wraps it and places it on the box with my other items. A small, satisfied smile graces his face.

"The store and I are ready to clear the stock. I'm going to post an all-stock must-go, pay what you can, one-day sale." Sal taps away on his phone. "Do you have access to The Nexus?"

"The what?"

"The essence social media, it's better than anything the ordinaries have."

"No, I don't."

"We'll get you on there. We use it for everything."

I'm struck by how much more vibrant Sal becomes with each passing moment. The store has yet to accept anything but fears becoming obsolete by clinging to the past. While I long to comfort and reassure it that is impossible, it isn't. It's almost guaranteed to happen.

Within twenty minutes, the store is rammed with customers, all purchasing something. My box and a few random items Sal collected together are stored under the desk, but everything else is up for grabs.

I run around the chaos and flood of people, rearranging and restocking with whatever I find in the storeroom. It's hot, sticky, hard work. Retail is no joke or walk in the park. Unless that park is an overcrowded, sweltering inferno full of grumpy bargain-hunters moaning as they crawl through the mob to get the last deal.

As quickly as the chaos started, it ends with the final item being sold. I let my back slide down the wall, not caring that I'm probably leaving a yukky trail of sweat, and accept the bottle of water Sal offers.

"Wow, that was... something else." I fan my face with my hand.

"It was. Don't tell anyone, but," his bottom hits the floor next to me, and he points at an enormous landscape with a thick gold frame opposite us. We stare at it, then each other. My ironic British sense of humor finds such an imposing item being missed hilarious, and I burst out laughing, Sal, too, although I feel this is more because he seems to be losing yet more of the shadow that has shrouded him into near obscurity.

Ten

I leave Sal to clean up and get reacquainted with the store. I'm more hopeful they'll make some decisions about their futures.

Needing to clear my head and feel some fresh air on my face, I wander to the beach. Several people stop to thank me for helping Sal and the store, all enquiring how they could support him. Some talk to me almost reverently, as if I'm someone truly special.

Echoes of the Merchant being whispered follow and float around me, gradually soaking in and filling a mysterious lifetime void.

Finding a seat, I collapse with a long huff and wait for the calming motions of the tide to ease my tattered nerves and chase away the chatter of people bickering over who gets to buy what.

Neither happens, and I suspect they won't until I'm ready to fully consider what the Merchant is. An impatient meow at my feet catches me by surprise and a colossal, wiry cat with dark amber eyes jumps onto my lap, grunts at me, turns around, brushing her bottom close to my face, flops down, and snores. The oddly grumpy, rumbly noise vibrates through me.

"Mommy, can we stroke Bluebell?" An excited child calls from the beach.

"Let me see how cranky she is today." Paige ruffles her son's hair and heads in my direction. "Kids, do not eat the sand again."

"My Ruby was a sand eater." I grin at her, marveling at how the hours we spent watching Ruby like a hawk are now a distant, fond memory. Paige sits beside me, keeping an eye on her children. Her usually bright energy is dimmed, and she twists the ring on her finger. "What's up?"

"Dray might be home for good." She shakes her head and closes her eyes. I switch my line of sight from her to the sweet little duo. Austin has mischief practically printed over every inch of him, while mini-Paige, Emma stands over him doing all she can to ensure his sandcastle meets her standards.

"Is that a bad thing?" They don't seem to have any other family, and Whispering is a fantastic place. I cannot imagine

Draven's future being in a bookstore, but there has to be loads of things he could do.

"No, it's good." She turns toward me. "I'd love to have him home, and the kids adore him, and he's great with them. Everything you want an uncle to be and more, but..."

She trails off; I cast a quick look in her direction and watch as she tilts her head back, staring at the sky.

"I don't know why he returned." A tear glistens in the corner of her eye. "Something is wrong, it has been since The Adjustment, but he won't talk about it."

Before I can ask more, the children sprint to us, stopping about a foot from me. Paige plasters a big smile on her face and holds up her hand to them.

She reaches over and very cautiously runs a finger over the giant cat who has made me her bed. She huffs in her sleep, but otherwise does nothing.

"One at a time and only for a second." She draws her son close, holding his hand, ready to yank him away if need be. I poise, ready to restrain Bluebell. "Remember, gently and only once."

Bluebell makes no acknowledgment of the children, who soon return to building sandcastles.

"They'll be full of that for days." She ruffles Bluebell's head, screaming slightly when she snarls a menacing hiss.

"Bluebell. That's naughty." I exclaim to the cat, who snorts.

"I should know better." Paige shrugs. "I've got just about enough time to get them home before they decide they're too hungry and tired to walk and throw a hissy fit on the street."

"I'll walk with you." Staying still and watching the water has done nothing to soothe my swirling thoughts. Physical activity might, I also want to probe her for information.

Paige packs the beach toys in a canvas bag painted with flowers she purchased from Sal. We traipse behind the children, who mutter about Bluebell. She's a local celebrity. Stroking her without getting bitten is considered a sign of good luck, and if you don't even get hissed at, it's an honor.

"Earlier, you mentioned The Adjustment; what does that mean?"

"It was not the same for everyone, it affected different people in different ways." Paige says carefully, quietly, and when I'm convinced she isn't going to say more, she continues. "I believe those of us on Whispering were protected from the full impact it had on others. Some essence people experienced a sudden and profound change. A friend of mine, in The Faraway, had her appearance revert to how faes used to look thousands of years ago. Another lost her mental link to the pack. It changed a lot of folks like that. For a few, it completely altered their kismet, which is bad. Truly horrible."

"How had I not heard about this?" I stop dead, full of horror, even though I don't fully understand what any of that really means. We've all heard loads about the kismet being a fundamental part of all essence people.

"The media likes to report us in awful ways, but not when anything dreadful happens to us. At the time, the EA was playing down the explosion in Rock Falls and didn't want any more negative publicity, and they squashed the story as well."

"But people have to understand what happened to them." For some strange reason, I nearly said my people.

"Most of us only experienced something minor like when a brand replaces its logo or when you paint a room a near identical color. It was nothing to worry about, and we simply moved on. The kismet has the ability to grow and learn. It evolves. It makes millions of tiny modifications every single day. A new alpha here, mates finding each other there. Two packs combining. All those are minor alterations within the kismet. The difference was that, on this occasion, we all felt something."

"That must be difficult for you all." I want to use a stronger term and maybe even rant at how unfair that is, but I bite my tongue.

"Um. Ginny, you do realize that you..."

"Paige, what is Austin eating?" Gran appears from nowhere, holding her hand out in front of the little boy, who defiantly shakes his head.

"Spit it out." Paige kneels before him, prying his mouth open. "Oh, crap, it's another dirty stone. He'll end up with worms again."

"I told him not to, Mommy, but he does it anyway." I crack a grin at Emma's indignation and Austin's refusal to give up his prized stone.

"Good girl. Next time, tell me, though." Paige inspects the red teeth marks on her finger after prying the stone from Austin's mouth, who now has big fat tears threatening to roll down his cheeks.

"Austin, I do not want to have to take another worming tablet." Emma declares very loudly, making heads turn, and Paige goes bright red. "You should suck your thumb."

"No!" Paige takes an audibly calming breath, holding up her son's hand for Emma to see. "What I mean is, his fingers are no cleaner than the stones."

"Reminds me of the twins." Gran chuckles alongside me.

"Kids, Ice cream. Now." Paige stands up, almost dragging Austin into a tiny ice cream shop. I follow, wondering why the urgency for a treat.

"Not again." Emma stamps her foot, crossing her arms over her chest, refusing to enter.

"Emma!" Paige calls, settling Austin into a highchair. The little girl ambles in and sulkily takes a seat.

"Two of the normal." Paige sighs to the cheery older gentleman behind the counter, who looks like Santa Claus on vacation. He goes out the back and returns with two lime green ice creams and covers them in chocolate sauce and sprinkles before placing them in front of the unimpressed kids.

"The ice cream has a potion woven through it to help prevent children from developing stomach bugs or worms. Your father ate it by the bucket load." Gran has only mentioned him once, and that was to tell me I was better off without him after I asked when I would see him. I was four, but I remember her disgust as if it was yesterday.

"I'm going to help Paige get the kids to eat it. Will you be free later? I have some questions."

"I'll stop by with dinner." Then she's gone. My gaze darts up and down the road, but Gran is nowhere to be seen.

By getting the children to tell me about their favorite places on the island, we got them to eat every spoonful of 'the icky,' as Emma called it. I'm meeting them at the park on Saturday, and if Austin can refrain from putting anything he shouldn't in his mouth, I will treat them to their bestest burger and fries. His words and choice.

I didn't get any more from Paige, but Gran is due shortly. Wanting the meal to feel relaxed and not like the interrogation bursting inside me, I lay the table on the deck. Adding a chilled bottle of wine and a jug of iced water. Plus, a few citrus candles to keep the bugs away, not that they're much of an issue.

"The house feels more you with each second." Gran's warm approval wraps around me and my little cottage. "It let me in."

"I see." I'd prefer to know when people arrive rather than have the house just grant them entry.

"No, you don't, but that is all to be expected." Gran empties several food containers from a stay-warm bag and places them in the center of the table. "I can explain as we have dinner."

"I need to understand more than just the house. Like The Adjustment and the Merchant." I seize my opening and run with it.

"I see. I'll fill in what gaps I'm able." She pours wine and uncovers the deliciously aromatic duck, vegetables, and roast potatoes, dishing it up for us.

I sit and follow her lead in eating. "Wow." It's sublime. "How is all the food so good?"

"Magic."

"Really?" I hold the forkful I was about to put in my mouth and squint at it.

"It's proper food, but the chefs can enhance the taste as they prepare it. Good becomes great, but unpleasant becomes diabolical. They still need talent."

"Has that changed since The Adjustment?" Persistence pays with Gran. She sips her wine, and I get her assessing stare. As a child, it scared me rigid and still does to an extent, but not as much as not getting answers.

"The Adjustment affected everything essence and kismet wise. However, the effects on Whispering were far more muted than for The Faraway. Though, it destroyed your aunt Valeria's relationship with the Emporium and strengthened her wanderlust. Her desire to see The Faraway was stronger than her call to stay. The house and store were deserted as a result."

"Is the Emporium a store anyone can walk in and buy what they want?" I ask, already knowing the answer. It's set too far away from the others. How uninviting the obscured glass and windowless door are strikes me with a slap.

"There is considerably more to the Emporium than one person will ever be capable of comprehending." Her tone and eyes border on resentful. Her bangles jangle as she waves her hands. "There are many such places on Whispering, each with a unique purpose and history, maybe none as veiled as the Emporium. It is believed to have been the first thing on the island, and the source of Whispering's exceptional nature. As I understand it, the Merchant and her team are charged with the care and rightful re-homing of sensitive or consequential essence artifacts."

"Define sensitive or consequential essence artifacts."

"No one speculates on such things, Ginny." Gran chastises me with a stern glare. "That is the business of the Merchant and her helpers."

"But, Gran, you have me running the Emporium, living in the Merchant's house. How is that speculation?" Damn my voice for rising. "Please, help me understand."

The silence stretches as Gran lays her cutlery on the plate and straightens her pale pink, wrap sundress. Panic that she doesn't know anything and honestly thinks I'm here to help in a shop drives a cold, sharp blade into my soul.

"Don't worry, I'll ask Delly." I sigh, unable to reconcile the innocent woman having anything to do with something sinister.

"You can't." Gran pushes her plate to the side and sits forward. "Delly is only front store staff. Whether that was different before the incident, I..."

I don't bother to push Gran when her voice trails off; I don't need to. Her fear says it all. Something happened to Delly at the Emporium, and it was bad enough to change her as a person. Her exuberance and almost child-like manner now make more sense than I want them to.

"I was very young when Valeria became the Merchant, too little for anyone to care what I heard. From what I recall and bits I have pieced together since, the Merchant has always been from our family. Valeria was trained for many years by the Merchant who came before her, as they had been for eons. Their role is, or partly, to give the right item to the right person or Seeker at the right time."

I think about the silver tankard I secured from Sal's store. It's waiting for the right person to come for it. Seeker has a familiar ring to it.

"There are people who bring items. I'm sure I heard them called Procurers. I have never met one, or at least not knowingly."

"How would I find them?" A cautious spark of hope that there is someone who knows what to do and I may not be alone springs to life.

"It has only been Valeria and Delly for some years." The spark dwindles and fades away.

"How dangerous is it?" My voice, like my spirit, is as flat as a pancake.

"Why would it be dangerous?" Gran all but rolls her eyes at me.

"A simple closed sign will not prevent someone determined to possess a sensitive or consequential essence artifact they should not have."

"I... That was not..." Gran shakes her head, alarm shooting from her aura.

"I'll help, but the Merchant is bigger than me." I give her hand a squeeze and clear the plates. Gran follows me in and packs the leftovers into the fridge, her shoulders tense, and frequent audible breaths betray how worried she is. The odd glimpse I get of the myriad of expressions flying over her face pulls on my heartstrings.

"I would be grateful if you could keep the store and house company until a better candidate comes along." Gran tells me, giving me a dejected, disappointed sort of look.

"I can do that." I loathe to see Gran dismayed, but I'm not the person she needs. "Why do you need to find someone?"

"It is our heritage all the way back to The Ancestor, but it might be time to look outside the family."

"The Ancestor?" Is there no end to the cryptic terms people are going to casually throw at me as if I have a single clue about any of them? Although I have a niggling feeling she's doing it on purpose to deter me.

"You'll know who he is if you ever meet him." She smiles sadly.

We finish the bottle of wine, talking about my disappointingly sketchy plans for my future. I'm forty-one, old enough to have some inkling of how to spend the rest of my life and young enough to make it happen. It doesn't matter that my back is killing me and my knees are screaming, even after I've taken several Advil. I refuse to accept the best years are behind me.

Eleven

After a restless night of tossing and turning with little actual sleep, a few things are very clear to me. First, is a special role that has been honored for millennia. Second, it's time to tell my sister my marriage is over and why. I email her to call me when she can, telling her what time zone I'm in. I then message the twins to check-in. Owen will reply when he sees it, Ruby, whenever she feels like it.

I take a cup of tea into the garden and settle to watch the new day dawn. My mental to-do list builds in my mind far quicker than I want it to. I enjoy the sense of purpose but not the constant, gnawing fear I'm missing something.

With my tea drunk and the sun peeking over the horizon, I head to my, no, the Emporium to continue the cleaning. Starting where I left off with Percy, I stare at the thimble, still wanting to free his essence. The unwelcome prospect that I'll never be able to do that because I am not the Merchant screeches through me.

I clean and rearrange while refusing to consider the history of anything in the store, making the task much quicker, and I finish the shelves before lunch. I open the door to let some air in and turn the fan to the chair so I can cool off as I enjoy an ice lolly.

It's strange no one comes in. They don't even peer through the window. I flop back and bring my legs to curl under me. The itchy compulsion to understand everything about this eccentric little place wrenches all my denials into a solid ball that could easily be kicked to the sun and incinerated.

"You got a moment?" Sal lingers by the door, half huddled in on himself.

"Course. Want one of these?" I wave my lolly, and he nods. I go to fetch him one. When I get back, he has not moved. "You can come in."

"I can?" He hesitantly steps through inside, his expression stuck between surprise and awe. "It's so cute."

The store rumbles beneath our feet. "Sorry, I meant impressively fascinating," Sal calls, and the quaking stops.

"Haven't you been inside before?"

"Goodness, no." Sal shakes his head, taking everything in. "No one was invited in unless the store granted their request."

The questions punch into my mind but remain unspoken; I am not the Merchant; I do not need to understand.

"How are you?" Yesterday, although therapeutic and necessary, would not have been easy for him.

"Okay. Not great, but not terrible." Which matches how he looks. He and his clothes are clean, but he lacks the aura of someone at ease with his life. I ignore how I can suddenly see auras and refuse to debate why. Yes, I am denying a lot of things, but ho hum.

"That's progress."

"It is." He parks himself on the very edge of the sofa. "The store might be agreeing to become a learning center. Would you be able to ask it for me?"

"I will, but I need to make sure you understand I am not the Merchant."

"I fully accept that you believe you are not and accept the risk that you may not be."

"What makes you think I might be?" We'll call this curiosity and not a burning necessity to stay where I am and shower the Emporium with protective care and devotion.

Sal sits back, cocking his head to the side, regarding me carefully. I wait for him to agree that I'm not and leave to search for someone else to help.

"You have the right qualities and essence. The Merchant's house and the store welcomed you. I don't think. I know." He stands and bows. "See you when you're ready."

A GENIE'S NEW START

Then he's gone, leaving me to gawk after him with my mouth hanging open. I have an essence? Me?

My genie lamp shines from its perch, trapping my gaze and commanding me to submit to its protection. I'm on my feet and taking the first unsteady step on that fateful journey to blighted devotion when my phone rips my attention away. I grab it and hurry outside to answer.

"Hi."

"You sound like you've run a marathon. What did I interrupt?" Lea's welcome brand of sense is what I need. If anyone can make sense of this, it's my best friend, even if she is thousands of miles away in the UK.

"I'm a genie, and I was about to go back to my lamp." I blurt. "But I'm not The Merchant, but everyone seems to want me to be, including the store and house. The food has fat and calories but is so good because of magic. The giant cat who could scare a tiger is called Bluebell, and Percy is stuck in a thimble."

Because, apparently, telling her I'm a genie wasn't enough.

"I... that's... What?" Lea stutters at me.

"You're lost for words. You're never lost for words. This is all bad, isn't it?" I perch on a bench and wave at a wolf walking past, dipping his head at me. "I just waved at a wolf, a big gray one."

"Ginny, whatever you're taking or drinking needs to stop." Lea hisses. "You can't lecture the twins then do it yourself."

"I'm not. This is all real."

"How?!"

"Remember all the essence and kismet stuff on the news that's too far-fetched to be real?"

"Yeah."

"Well, not only is it real, but it's only the tip of the iceberg."

"I see." I hear her taking deep breaths as she paces. "Are you safe? You mentioned a wolf."

"He's a shifter. There are loads on the island."

"I'm going to glaze over the food because I'm waiting for dinner to finish cooking and too hungry. Who is Percy, and how is he stuck in a thimble?"

"He's a merman, and a witch put his essence there. No one has discovered how to free it."

"What else would he be? Who or what is the Merchant, and why is it not you?"

"It can't be. I'm a married mother of two in my forties." I remind her because no one can see this.

"You are a single, awaiting a divorce, woman in her prime. Your children are grown up and independent. Forty is the new twenty but with common sense and life experience. I need another good reason why you cannot claim your future as the Merchant." I picture her resolutely setting her shoulders.

"I don't know what the Merchant is," I sag. "But it isn't me. I am not the Merchant."

"Wait, did you say you're a genie? As in grant wishes and disappear into thin air?" Her excitement is contagious, but it always is. Lea is the person who makes a gathering a party.

"I believe I am. My gran is a genie, and I have a lamp that I shouldn't touch, but I can't not." I swallow the lump in my throat that threatens to burst into another news dump.

"Promise me you'll get someone to lock it away." Lea's sharp tone is the one she uses when she will not take no for an answer. She'll call me every thirty minutes until I give up and do it.

"I promise to find out if that's possible." I concede, glad it won't be where I can see it. "What did you call for?"

There's a long pause, and I'm sure her breath catches. "To check-in. I miss you." Before I can ask what's really going on, she tells me dinner is ready and hangs up. Midday here is the middle of the night in the UK. If she's cooking this late, she either got caught up writing, which is completely possible, it happens a lot, or something is wrong. I'll message her tomorrow at a more UK-friendly time.

A shadow falls over me, blocking the fierce sun. I look up to see Draven staring down at me.

I would stand, but it would bring us very close together. My girlie bits and I perk up at the prospect until I remember he mum-zoned me.

"You seemed upset."

I shimmy along and get to my feet, not drinking in his bulging muscles rippling under his white sports top.

"I'm a genie." The air rushes from me, and my legs turn to jelly. I lunge forward, and Draven crushes me against his chest. His fresh ocean scent filters into my lungs. He rubs my back, and my nipples burst to life. I reluctantly pat his side to break his hold before I embarrass myself in front of him again. "Sorry, I didn't mean to..."

I don't have the foggiest inkling of what I didn't mean, and I open and close my mouth like an idiot school girl with a crush.

"To have your life spun on its head several times in a few weeks? Find out things about yourself you never imagined? Be charged with saving a man's entire future? Attempting to comprehend that stores have feelings that need to be abided by?" He smirks, his silver-gray eyes dancing.

"You missed my genie lamp wanting me back." I joke, despite it not being funny. Draven snaps to attention, his body tensing to laser-focused.

"It can't have you." He puts his hands on my waist, carries me outside, and shuts the door. "Stay."

I balk at his order but do it anyway. "What if it promises to behave?"

"Ginny, it needs to be locked away. It's dangerous." Inside, he reaches under the counter, lifts a small iron box, and places his index finger on the clasp. It falls open, revealing an ornate, black key that floats into his hand.

"Draven, let me in!" I bang on the glass and yank the handle, but it doesn't move, not even a tiny bit. The handle warms under my hand until it burns, forcing me to let go and watch in horror, he uses the key to unlock the dark cupboard, exposing my precious lamp to the terrors within. He carelessly shoves items aside to make space, all so he can conceal my lamp from me. The key goes back into the box, the door opens and I stomp in, thrusting my hands on my hips. "I can see where you put the key."

"But only the Emporium can grant you access to it." He tucks the box back under the counter. "It only grants it to the Merchant or her team."

"Then why you?"

"I used to help your aunt before I went to the academy. I guess the store remembers me." Aware that I'm standing like a toddler throwing a tantrum, I ease my shoulders.

"Thank you." A chill sweeps down my spine into my feet, almost dragging me outside. "Are you making the store throw me out?"

"No one gains entry unless the Emporium allows it. And it only does that if they have a purpose for being inside. It deems you as no longer having a purpose." Draven picks up my bag and follows me out.

"But why? I've been looking after it for days?" Big, angry, barren tears spill from my eyes. "My husband, my daughter, and now my own store. Why am I not good enough for anyone?"

I grab my bag and run. Crying is useless, a waste of time and energy. Whenever my mother ever caught me, she'd take a slipper to my backside, telling me I had something to cry over. I'm almost home when I realize it's connected to the store, and I may also be homeless.

The possibility of not sleeping in my own bed, baking in my own kitchen, or relaxing in my own garden makes me sob harder.

My front door flies open, and I dart in, dramatically falling on my sofa and wailing into my arms.

I'm woken by claws digging into my back that I would ignore if my eyes and throat weren't coated in sand.

"Good evening." My gran puts a cup of tea and tissues in front of me. I sit up, blow my nose, and sip my drink, feeling very sorry for myself as I wait for her to tell me I must leave the island. Bluebell sprawls over my lap, grunting in her sleep.

Gran has the silent treatment perfected. She makes it awkward and tedious all at once. As a kid, I lasted about three minutes before I confessed to whatever I'd done wrong.

"I haven't done anything wrong." I put my empty mug down and hug a grumpy Bluebell closer.

"No one said you had." Gran gracefully crosses one leg over the other and settles into the chair. "I am confused why you deny being the Merchant then instantly call this yours."

I shrug.

"Is the actual store too wretched?"

"No!" My head shoots up. "How could it be?"

"The house?"

"It's my home."

"The artifacts? Did Percy scare you that much?" I'm totally unimpressed with how much of the story she has.

"He did, but once I understood, it was fine. A warning that such things are possible would not have gone amiss. Now I need to find a way to free him." I cannot keep the accusation out of my voice, not that I really tried. "Why did you never tell me I was a genie?"

"Ahh..." Gran stares at a painting of the back of a blond man holding a purple book. "There was no benefit to telling you when the fact essence people existed was a secret. Revealing it meant death. I didn't want you in that position."

"Then after?"

"We can't do anything. Our powers were bound numerous centuries ago. The world has not been kind to essence people. Too many have been murdered in cold blood. After careful consideration, I believed it was the best way to keep you safe."

"But it's my heritage, Gran." I may completely understand her viewpoint and even agree to an extent, but it hurts. I wipe away more angry tears.

"One I longed to tell you." Her anguish rings through her words, drawing me to her. She meets me halfway, bestowing me with one of her magic hugs, the ones that always make anything okay. "Now you know I'll explain everything, but, first, we need to talk about the store, sweetheart."

I flop back on the sofa, wanting to blame hormones for my emotional state. My GP did tell me I was perimenopausal.

"Is Percy an essence artifact?" My swirling emotions have clumped unpleasantly together. Bluebell bats my hand, and I idly stroke her wiry, ginger neck.

"He is an example, but few have the actual essence of a person inside them. Most have trace magic or are charmed for a certain purpose or reason. They cannot be left where just anyone could potentially gain access to their powers."

"What powers? How would someone gain access?" My yearning to learn more intensifies with each second. It's pouring through my veins and every atom of my being, ready to engulf me.

"Those are questions to aim at the Merchant. Who will be gifted the answers to that and much more upon achieving the role." Gran leans forward, her entire demeanor unwavering.

"Am I capable?" My hushed tone is clearer than I wanted it to be. The house and Bluebell whine at me.

"Of course, my granddaughter is capable." Gran glares at me. I hadn't meant it as a personal disparaging remark. "However, being capable and fully accomplishing are very separate. There is a trial period in which the store, role, or house could reject you. And vice versa. You would not be the first to declare it was not for you."

"Why would anyone do that?"

Gran smiles at my bafflement. "Asks the child who already did."

"What do you mean, already did? Is it too late?" My chest constricts, and I choke back a sob.

"Shall we return to the Emporium and see?" She's out the door before I can even debate. I follow on stumbly legs that are certain they should not be holding me upright.

Twelve

Eyes bore into me from every angle as my audience watches me trail behind Gran with Bluebell by my side. I veer between knowing I am the Merchant to knowing I am not. Each step brings a thousand flashes of knowledge and fresh awareness of what the role entails. The adversarial side of the role, the doom and death, war with the sanctuary, and compassion of the good.

Many previous Merchants have succumbed to the dark or surrendered to the light. However, this isn't an enlightened to higher plane of calling situation; it's giving the wrong artifact to the wrong person because you felt sorry for them. Either leaving a true Seeker without what they should be granted or allowing evil to be released to a greater evil.

All of which serves to confirm the one thing that is unequivocally and steadfastly at the center of my thoughts; there is no good choice.

Gran stops at the border of the Emporium and ushers people away. They suddenly become consumed with whatever store window they're in front of. Except for Draven standing on the other border with his arms crossed over his chest, fiercely watching and waiting. I'd dearly love a clue to what he's thinking or feeling, but his face is devoid of expression.

A need beyond me or my doubts and fears, even past my wish to find a future to claim, propels me on. I quash my nausea and ignore the hairs standing on end.

A blind panic that the door won't open cascades through me. I'm clueless if this is right for me, but I'm not ready to lose it.

I fight the light-headed anticipation of reaching for the handle with deep breaths that are far more ragged than I want. The smooth, icy-cold metal twists grudgingly in my grasp. The door creaks with an ominous warning, and I send the store a silent but heartfelt apology.

I miss the warmth and welcome from every other time I've been here. Even Percy stares indignantly down at me. I take cautious steps to the center and turn slowly around, examining every inch and item.

"You into second chances?" I sound out, pushing through an invisible barrier to get behind the counter and try to pick up the cloth I used to clean, but it refuses to move. I close my eyes and tune into the Emporium, forcing my way through its reluctance to let me in. "Yes, I scorned you, and I apologize. But I'm midlife and have been made to feel over the hill and unworthy. Which I might be."

A harshly chilling breeze bites over my skin as the store's rejection of that slays me. "Can we try again?"

The air warms, the cloth floats into my hand, and Percy winks. I grin, trying to hide how freaked out I still am that an image painted onto a thimble can move.

Draven is dragged inside, his head darting around as I'm about to ask when I get a team. Delly follows a few seconds after.

"Welcome to the team." Delly cheers, and Draven looks like he swallowed a hornet's nest.

"I'll work hard; I will. I mop, scrub, and stock. Anything." Delly declares, lying over the counter, hugging it. Leaving big fingerprint streaks across the glass. "I start now with the lamps."

She plugs earphones into her ears, picks up a cloth, and gets to work.

"You don't want to be associated with the Emporium?" I regard Draven's ticking jaw and tight posture.

"It's not that." He grinds out. "The Emporium and I get along just fine."

"Then what?" The Emporium fears further rejection, and while I may not fully understand what the consequences are, I sense how the air has darkened. Draven shakes his head, growling slightly.

"It's personal."

"The same thing that brought you to Whispering?" Go this new bold-as-you-like me!

"I was born here. I have family here." His Adam's apple bobs among the corded muscles in his neck.

"But your life isn't or wasn't here. You mentioned the Academy, but you are not in a Guardian Team. Are you an Overseer?" Some of that I already knew, and some bursts into my mind in a not entirely fun way. The Academy is where the EA trains Guardians and Overseers. The Guardian Teams are small military teams who police the EA world in whatever manner they deem fit, from assistance to termination. The Overseers work individually, watching over essence people for various reasons, but, again, they offer anything from assistance to termination.

"I was." His top lip curls into a vicious sneer, exposing large, menacing fangs. My cutie is a sight to behold, foreboding, savage, and deeply demoralized.

"Now you're a Procurer. The Emporium has chosen you, but you must also choose." My voice is not my own. It's reinforced with power, kismet, and authority that goes beyond what could be achieved in a single lifetime, no matter how long that person has lived.

"I'm not right for a Procurer." Draven spins on his heel as scales cloak his skin and leathery wings rip from his back. He launches himself skywards the instant he is out of the door.

"He'll be back," Delly yells over her music. I nod at her, wishing I had her confidence in him.

Wanting some peace and a moment to regain my equilibrium, I flick my hand down, lowering the concealment over the Emporium because I've grasped I can.

I click the fan on and fetch two decadent chocolate-dipped ice cream cones.

"Delly, come and tell me what you do here?" She takes one and perches on the edge of the sofa, shuffling her feet, which is very distracting.

"I do whatever is needed."

"What position do you hold?" I persist.

"I never had a position. If there's work to do, I do it, if not, I don't." She starts taking huge bites from the ice cream.

"Slow down. You'll give yourself brain freeze. If we're sat down talking, it means there is something to do, and we're doing it. Okay?" I want her to understand she's valued, but without a deeper understanding of the roles, I'm limited in what I have to offer her. She nods and slows down, sitting back and swinging her legs. "Can you explain your relations with the store?"

She whimpers and curls in on herself. Alarm filling her eyes and voice. "It saved me. I repay it."

"Did someone tell you how long you needed to work here to do that?"

"I want to. Are you going to make me leave?" Her bottom lip quivers. I shake my head, and it stops.

"You are welcome here, but I'm not sure what will happen. We'll leave further talk about your future here until the future is clearer." And I have a shed load more details about what happened and how the store saved her without upsetting her by asking. "However, are you paid for the work you do?"

"I am." She nods almost frantically at me.

"Can you tell me about the Procurer?" The store's approval permeates through its caution.

"They get the stuff that does the stuff." Her huge toothy grin is made even more special by her pride.

"There's more than one?" Trying to keep my questions simple while still getting information is challenging. I long to drill her for specifics, but I don't think the store would like that any more than she could answer.

"Yes. Some are permanent, and others only deliver the odd thing. They carried on. There's stuff that needs to be cataloged." She darts to her feet and dances across the floor, pulling a book to open a concealed door.

"I guess I'd better learn how to catalog." I move to get a closer view and dozens of items stare back at me in a room that's location defies the laws of physics.

"I'm not allowed in there, though." Delly tilts her head down, looking at me through the tops of her eyes. "So, I don't touch."

"Good." I rub her arm and return to the chair. She closes the door and springs back to the sofa. "What do you feel I need to know?"

I get a moment of panic as her face lights up, and she gulps a huge breath. "First, Empy is upset but gets that you're scared."

"Sorry, who is Empy?"

"The Emporium," Delly tells me as though it's obvious. "Empy isn't pleased with Draven. His response unsettled her. They are friends."

"He may just need time," I tell Empy gently. Delly mumbles agreement around her ice cream. "Anything else."

"Danger is coming, big dangerous, evil danger." She inclines her head one way and then the other. "You need to be ready."

"What danger?"

"Dunno." She shrugs.

"How long do I have?"

"Dunno." She shrugs again. I put the horror movie vibe in a box and lock it.

"You have a close relationship with Empy." Delly sits straight, preening. I debate my next question, her attention is waning, and her shuffling has increased. "Does Empy tell you anything she wouldn't tell anyone else?"

Delly shakes her head emphatically, biting her lip so hard I see her tooth pierce the skin. "Whatever you don't want to say must be spoken."

"The stuff talks to me." She mutters quietly.

"What does it say?" I keep the order in my tone and command in my gaze.

"Mostly, nothing much, nothing more than a greeting." I intensify my stare. "Some bits want me to do things, not always good things."

"Thank you for telling me. As soon as that happens, you are to let me or Draven know, and we will deal with it."

"Okay."

"Delly, I need you to promise me and Empy." Empy sends a gust of frigid air around Delly.

"I promise. Can I clean now?"

"You may." Her earphones go back in, and she jigs while making everything spick and span.

Exhaustion descends on me, but I lift the concealment, thinking maybe I should have asked Delly how people find us or even what the opening hours are.

I told Delly to go home when she started singing along with her music, explaining I needed to visit Sal and prepare for Sunday. My ribs are still sore from her bear hug when I said I'd see her Monday.

Sal has a row of books on a shelf and boxes arranged around the space. Muttering to himself, he moves the boxes to the edge.

"How's it going?" I stay in the doorway, not wanting to slow his creative flow.

"Like trying to ride a horse upside down." He huffs. Carrying books from one wall to another. "Nothing is right."

"How about you?"

"The same."

"You're looking much better." I'm able to make out the color of his eyes, features, and even his aura is clearer.

"You mean you can actually see me now, not just a shadow?" He scrubs his hand over his face. "Thanks for being there and seeing me as a person."

"Anytime." I wander past him, patting his arm, trying to tune into the store. It's withdrawn considerably, overwhelmed with the sudden change. "Sal, take the rest of today and tomorrow off, catch up on anything else you want or need to do, and we'll tackle it afresh Sunday."

"What's the plan?" Sal retrieves a lunch pail from the back room.

"That's a splendid question. I'm open to ideas." I run my finger along a shelf, hoping for inspiration.

"A memorial service."

"Do you mean to help the store move on?" I don't wait for his response because it is not merely the store that needs that stepping stone. "That might be a good idea. People have ceremonies for everything, so why not the store? That's what we'll do Sunday. Can you make an announcement on The Nexus? The ceremony to be followed by a refurb."

"Sure. How will that work?"

"Guess we'll all find out together. See you there." I stride away as Sal mutters to himself and the store. They are nowhere near in tune, but the slow mutual descent of deathly oblivion has faded.

Sera holds up two almost identical dresses in front of a shapely woman with flowing, flaxen hair, who turns her nose up and gives her a dirty look. "I said I wanted sexy."

"These are sexy, verging on slutty. You want to be a slut?" I choke a shocked laugh at her exasperated question.

"Yes, you know I do, sis." The woman motions under the bust line of the shorter dress, a bright red, almost see-through lace. "Can we do cut-outs? Showing some boobage?"

"You take it to Aunt Mavis and ask her." Sera thrusts the frock at her and drags her inside. I follow, more than a little curious. Also, some of the pieces in their window are lovely.

"Aunt Mavis, can we slutify this?" The flaxen-haired beauty calls, disappearing through a door at the back. Sera sighs, putting the other dress on a rack and smoothes non-existent wrinkles from her cream blouse. They appear to be even more different than the twins, and I never believed that was possible.

"Slutify?" I chuckle when she rolls her eyes.

"It's the same every month. She comes in for something for a throng that she'll wear for twenty minutes before she strips and..."

"Shags?" I supply because Sera is too busy shuddering to speak.

"Baby sisters are meant to be sweet and wholesome. Not a..."

"Shifter caught in the monthly hormone surges?" Is called from the door before it slams.

"She's my baby sister." Sera cringes.

"I see your baby sister with the monthly uncontrollable hormone surges and raise you." I pull out my phone and bring up a photo of Rose with the twins. She's instantly recognizable to anyone, even if they've lived under a rock with no media for several decades.

"She's your sister?" Sera gawks at me, which is a far more common reaction than it should be. "Her? Rose Thorn? The..."

"Yes, but she's really, um, she's a good sister and aunt." I was going to call her sweet, but that is a lie, she's as prickly as her name suggests. But she is a great sister and aunt.

"Do not tell my little brother when she visits." Sera's eyes dart to the door as she mouths. "Please."

"I'm not sure Whispering has the right atmosphere for her." She's more suited to war zones and trendy nightclubs.

"Your gran is related to Rose Thorn?" Sera's grin is full of mischievous mirth.

"Technically." Their relationship is complex enough to keep a therapist busy for several lifetimes.

"I feel better." Sera chuckles, laying out a pen and notebook. "You here for your Merchant gear?"

"I..."

"You are," she unrolls a tape measure, indicates for me to lift my arms, and starts taking my measurements. "You won't know you are, but you are. It's one step in the process. Nice waist-to-hip ratio."

"Huh... thanks." I'm not overly hung up on my body, but I am forty-one and carried twins, but who wouldn't love hearing that?

"Next, you need to pick a color. Black is popular but overdone. Red is too bright. Gray is dull, and brown will make you look like a tree trunk. Green, pink, white, and yellow are nos." She points to a wall of fabric still on the roll. "Purple or purple and black.

She lugs over two large rolls of purple leather and spreads them out on an empty table in the middle of the store. Then gets a black roll and plonks it between them.

"Sera, I am not wearing leather. I'll bake." I declare, fetching my choice. A pretty, pale blue cotton with a pink and white floral pattern cascading over it.

"Knives and swords will go through that easier than butter," she dismisses it, "but it'll make a nice summer dress, bring out your eyes."

"Knives?" I try really hard to lose the shrillness of my voice. "Swords?"

Sera freezes, swallowing. "Ignore me. We'll make you a lovely summer dress. Sleeveless? Vest sleeves? Cap sleeves? Long, short, mid?"

"Stop!" I halt her barrage. "What knives and swords?"

Her shoulders deflate, and she lets out an audible breath. "Not everyone who comes to the store has good intentions. Some of the items you have in there cannot fall into the wrong hands and need to be defended. That's where your training in armed combat will come in."

"What training?" The room spins, and my chest constricts. I can't stop shaking my head.

"Oh. Maybe it'll be in the legacy wisdom."

"Really?" I don't want to use a knife or a sword. I can't even contemplate holding one, but exactly how did I think I would stop someone who was trying to obtain something they shouldn't have? I'm going to need to be able to defend it.

"Sure." Sera hides her grimace and climbs a step to lift a dusty roll of dark purple leather from the top shelf. "This will be for you."

I run my hand over the coarse, unyielding fabric. The unpleasant brown undertone adds to the lack of appeal.

"I really don't think I'll need to wear this, but thanks, anyway. Can I just order the summer dress?" I shake my head, refusing to contemplate a situation where I'll require the level of protection this heavy, rigid leather provides.

"Sure, let me get the pattern book for you."

Thirteen

I trudge away, keeping my head down to avoid anybody from seeing the thoughts spiraling around my mind.

Each second takes my life further from anything I can envision myself living. The future I intended to claim consisted of an interesting job, a nice little house, and people I enjoyed being with. Not battles with deadly weapons and hostile situations.

How I got to this is a strange jumble of events and half-truths. Bluebell meows up at me and falls into pace. I arrive home and dump a tin of tuna in a bowl for her. She gobbles it then finds a spot in the garden to snooze.

I fix an iced soda and settle onto the sun lounger under the parasol. Putting aside the midlife mum of two aspect, I am not the person to wield a knife or sword. Playing pretend lightsaber battles with the twins used to be fun, and we each got quite good at countering moves, but this is a universe away from that.

I was devastated when I left a massive bruise on Owen's arm. He cheered me on, and Lawrence merely asked if Ruby was okay. But seeing an angry black and purple mark on my child that I'd caused was too much for me. I told the twins they were broken and donated them.

A real sword could take a life, end it completely, and I would be responsible. A killer.

Am I capable?

I answer my phone, without thinking, to my sister's irritating voice. "You left him and didn't call me to party."

"It wasn't a party situation."

"Then what was it?" I nearly tell her the truth but stop myself. Her vicious streak is a mile wide, and I've never been sure she was joking when she said her friend's pigs would eat a body if we wanted to dispose of one.

"Perfectly friendly and amicable."

"Then it won't be awkward if I visit him for dinner tonight as planned?"

"Do not do that. He had an affair."

"Yes, he did, but don't worry, I put bromide in his coffee."

"Rose, please tell me you didn't." I cry out, causing Bluebell to whine at me.

"I didn't. Where are you, anyway?" I hear her moving around and putting clothes on.

"Whispering with Gran. Have you just got home?"

"Why else would I be changing at 5am? What's the island like?"

"Magical. Literally." A person with wings flies over me and disappears into the distance.

"Sounds interesting." Her code for not worth bothering with. She yawns down the line and apologizes profusely. Her secret fear is that people will think she's boring. As if.

"Sis, get some sleep and call me."

"'Kay, night." She hangs up, and I stare at my phone, deliberating if I should check what she did to Lawrence. I once caught her crushing Viagra into his dinner when his mother was visiting. Her excuse was that he was a meanie and her gaze darted to Owen.

Rose would tell me that anyone, including me, could take a life then come up with imaginative and undisputable scenarios.

The following day brings glorious sunshine, stomach cramps, and a craving for chocolate. Giving me something to blame for my tears yesterday.

The miserable decision to get out of bed is eventually won by my bladder and the longing to brush my teeth. I stumble into elasticized waist shorts and plod downstairs. My cranky search for ibuprofen ends with a weary sniffle when I recall where I am, and the Advil I'm holding is what it's called in the US.

I swallow them and get the Acetaminophen ready for a bit later, grab the huge bar of chocolate I brought with me, and flop onto the sofa. After a far too stressful fight to make the remote control work, I settle on watching an ancient black and white movie. After thirty minutes, just as the main character is about to lose her husband and children to illness, I switch it off. Kill off the man, fine, but not the babies. Now I can pretend a gorgeous hunk of a man swooped in to save them and won her love from the unworthy husband.

By lunch, my cramps subside enough for me to feel guilty and conscious about how much chocolate I ate. I draw in my stamina and summon my patience because perimenopausal hormones are a bitch and brave the outside world for a walk. My intention is to stroll along the cliff but sliding into a booth in the 1950s-style diner, I face admitting I failed.

Not feeling sociable, I pull out my phone and pretend to read.

"She's reading on a phone, can you believe that?" Paige slides in across from me.

"When you have so many books you need to clear from the store? No, I cannot." Harley follows her.

"I was pretending because I'm hormonal, bloated, and about to pig out on burger and cake." I sigh.

"Hugs. We're only here for lunch, then we'll leave you to wallow." They start discussing food options, and I realize I haven't ordered. Great customer I am. I decide on the pulled pork steak burger and death by quadruple chocolate cake with cream and chocolate shavings.

"If I'm going to feel like I swallowed and then inflated a beach ball, I want it to be worthwhile. Anyway, no one will see me naked." I defend myself when they try not to stare at me with wide eyes.

"Don't tell my brother." Paige snorts. "Where is he, by the way?"

"Tied to your bed?" Harley waggles her eyebrows at me.

"Eww, that's my brother." Paige sticks her tongue out at Harley, who laughs.

"I haven't seen him since early yesterday." I ignore their comments about my cutie and I. Harley is much more his type of woman, at least he wouldn't mum-zone her.

"He'll turn up." Harley loses all joviality and assures Paige, who nods with a worried, false smile.

"What's going on?" A truly weird concern about his welfare niggles into my core, and it's strange because it has no basis in any of the interactions I've had with him.

"He's been through a lot, and, yesterday, when he left the store, his aura was..." Paige broke off and looks around to see several listening in. "Different."

"Oh." I swallow the explanation. It isn't mine to give. Our drinks arrive, and I seize the opportunity to move the topic away from Draven. "Where's the best place to order refreshments for everyone helping tomorrow?"

"The other store holders already have seen to that." Harley dismisses and waves her hand through the air. "Now, I have a sound barrier in place so no one can hear. How different?"

"How do you do that?" I mimic her hand action as it flashes in my mind, she's a witch, and it was a spell. "That is cool."

"And useful. His aura was similar to our girl, here." Paige points to me, and Harley zooms in on yours truly with an intensity befitting an inquisition.

"I hate not seeing auras." She squints at me, and I can't help but chuckle at her staunch concentration. "Nope, nothing. Not a damn thing. What's going on?"

"I can't see it, either." I shrug, grinning when she rolls her eyes.

"There's the..."

"Do not give the colors and patterns." Harley blurts in. "Each time you do, I'm left none the wiser. I want cold, hard facts and emotions." Paige opens her mouth, but Harley isn't done. "Or the warm, squishy ones."

"What I can see is a whole lot of indecision and self-doubt, followed by a growing sense of duty. Good enough?" She aims at Harley.

"Not really, but it's a starting point." Her gaze swings to me. "Why self-doubt?"

I swallow because since they sat down, I've tried to decide in which scenarios I could and would kill to keep them safe. All while trying to remember this is real. Not a fantasy or story but my actual life, and it would end someone else's.

"We can and will hound you every second of every day until you tell us," Paige tells me matter-of-factly.

"I believe you. Is the sound barrier still up?" Harley nods. "I popped into Sera's store for some new clothes, and she measured me for a leather suit to keep me from getting wounded against the knives and swords. The doubt is if I could take a life."

"If you couldn't, the store would have rejected you already. Next doubt." Harley sips her strawberry milkshake.

"Let us settle a few." Paige crosses her arms. "Not enough knowledge about essence stuff. It'll appear in your head when you need it as if by magic. A woman commanding those big, bad, sexy as sin Procurers, Overseers, and maybe even Guardian Teams, the kismet will provide the authority as if by magic."

"No idea how to provide the Seekers with what they need," Harley takes over. "The store will step in and, as if by magic, you'll know."

"As if by magic?" I ask with something between a pained sigh and a huff.

"Guess what?" Paige waits for me to answer by giving tiny encouraging nods.

"Because it is all magic?" They clap and cheer. "But I am not magic."

"You are charmed. All genies are, and there's enough wizard and witch in your family." Harley points out, finishing her milkshake and holding up to request another.

I gape at her, open-mouthed. My mind is floundering so badly that I can't even snag the thought whizzing around it.

"You weren't aware?" The words are far away, underwater.

"Harley, call Rubaline."

"No way, you call her."

"She's not that scary."

"Great, then you call her."

"I'll call her." I snap out of it, dial, then stop and send her a message.

I'm a genie, witch, and wizard?

Who told you?

Am I?

Yes and no. Those essences are in the family line, but I cannot trace them in you.

I breathe again, not sure why being a witch or a wizard feels as momentous when I am a genie.

Our food arrives, and I eat, listening to Paige and Harley talking without taking anything in. They disappear when they finish eating, wishing me luck with my dessert. Leaving me glad I have them as friends because they were the distraction and reassurance I needed, but they also left me with a pounding headache.

I request my cake to go and amble home, avoiding people as much as possible. The privacy of home welcomes me with a comforting hug and melodic rumbling from the back garden.

I walk out, and Draven's dragon raises a sleepy eyelid, groaning. He's magnificent, a deep, rich blue with sharp scales running down his spine and wings spread out. I retrieve two spoons and my cake and lay on a lounger. The polystyrene container is big enough for a full meal and is stuffed to the brim with cake, cream, and chocolate. I soak in the heavenly aroma and hope it tastes as good. The dragon sniffs the air, almost purring. It's an addictive sound that could warm the water of Antarctica to tropical.

I put a spoonful into my mouth and whimper. It's divine. The dragon shuffles closer, laying his weighty head on my lap. I take the second spoon and feed him a large chunk. He swallows it, nudging my hand with his snout. The cake doesn't last much longer, but at least I was saved the calories. I show him the empty container. His pleading eyes would have worked if I had any left to give him.

A GENIE'S NEW START

"All gone." I chuckle as he perches on the edge of the lounger with a wing draped over me. The soft, leathery texture is cooling against the blazing afternoon sun. I gently rub his neck and take a minute of mindfulness against the surreal aspect of this moment.

I am lying with a dragon who becomes a stunning, muscular, kind man on an island that few people know exist, where the stores have emotions and purpose beyond earning money. The town hall changes each time I visit. I have friends who are supportive and fun, and I don't have to worry about keeping the fridge stocked just in case my daughter decides to raid it.

My freedom to experience all this came at a cost, but if I'm honest, I'd been pushing Lawrence away for a long, long time. Our sex life has been non-existent since we stopped trying for another baby. I long ago wrote that aspect of my life off for good. We should have divorced years ago, and the only reason I can come up with for still being together is habit for me and worry about what his mother would say about his part.

Fourteen

The dragon fades, and Draven's hard body is intimately pressed against mine. He cracks an eye open, and his slow, sexy grin takes my breath away.

Draven tugs me closer. I lick my dry lips, not able to tear my eyes from his as they hover over mine. My libido chooses this second to spring to life, screaming at me to kiss him and drag him fully on top of me. It doesn't last long, Draven soon wakes and jumps up, turning his back on me.

"Ahh, sorry about that. My dragon gets carried away when cake is involved. Just borrowing your bathroom." He zooms inside, and I curse myself for being a fool.

Do not get me wrong, I am in shape-ish and not unattractive, but Draven is book cover, swoon until you drool, and stick a fiver in his g-string if he was a stripper worthy. I chuckle, throwing the empty container away. He is worth much more than five pounds, but you gotta find the smallest paper denomination and spread that out. Is that why the US still has paper dollar bills? I could get five gropes here for five dollars, whereas it would only be one in the UK. Although, if I take the exchange rate into account, maybe even six or seven.

"What's so funny?" Draven leans against the door with one eyebrow raised, a small and very kissable grin lifting the edges of his perfectly plump and firm lips. I might have a problem.

"You had to be there." I open the fridge door and hide behind it, waiting for the cool air to chase away the awareness invading my system. It fails, and a bottle of ice cold water will have to do the trick. "Drink?"

He stands close behind me. His body heat invading my system and warm breath fanning my neck as he reaches past me to pull out a bottle of wine.

"We need to talk."

"Oh, goody." I shove past him and take a seat at the table. Waiting for whatever delight will follow.

"Is, we need to talk, code for something bad is about to be said?" Draven carries the wine and two glasses over, sitting opposite me.

"No, not at all. It's always something good." I retort, rolling my eyes. "So, what gleeful narrative did you have for me?"

"Gleeful narrative? What were you, an English major?" Draven shakes his head, twisting his lips, his eyes dancing.

"Minor, my major was history. My best friend is a writer, and when she's on a deadline, she'll call me for different ways to say the same thing."

"Remind me not to verbally spar with you. I wanted to talk about the store and roles."

"I see." The Emporium chooses that second to send an alarm, summoning me.

The hairs on the back of my neck stand on end as I obey the gut-wrenching need to judge the intentions of an unknown friend who could be a foe. I wave my hand, creating a hole in the fence and stride into Empy through a concealed door with Draven a step behind me. He retrieves a long, thick, silver sword and tucks it behind his back, where it disappears.

Silently, we enter the main part of our store, watching a man rifling under the counter, muttering to himself about being quick.

"Can we help you?" Draven drawls with a guttural edge, rising to his full, intimidating height. His dragon shimmering over his skin.

The man runs to the door, which closes, trapping him inside.

"The Emporium has granted you entry, meaning you have a purpose to be here, but summoned us, meaning it is not entirely honorable." This must be legacy knowledge, those words had not come to me until I spoke them.

"I.. umm.. let me explain." He stammers, picking up a large cannonball, and throws it at the window. It bounces back, stops inches from his face, and gently lands on the floor by his feet.

"Have we established you are confined inside until we allow you to leave?" My voice strengthens with power and authority. The same qualities pound my body with a calm readiness. He nods, frantically looking around. "Then, please, take a seat."

I point to the sofa and take my chair. He remains rooted to the spot.

"She said sit." Draven rumbles. The man flees to the sofa, shaking.

"Please explain your purpose and start with your name." I sense a small broach on the top shelf calling to go home. It has no real financial value, purely sentimental.

"Dylan. I need to present my mate's family with the broach that was stolen from them before I can claim her." Dylan leans forward, dejectedly resting his elbows on his knees and holding his head. "They gave me so much to do and buy, I ran out of money. I've saved to provide a home for my mate and family since I started work, but it wasn't enough. They promised this was the last, but I have..." He empties his pockets, laying some coins and a ten-dollar bill on the coffee table. "That."

"What are the family?" My anger blends with the Emporium's.

"Fae." Dylan slumps against the sofa, a cloak of pain and suffering darkening his aura.

"How long has this been going on for?" Draven's fury rings through his growl.

"About a year." He deflates. "They won't ever allow us to be together, will they?"

I retrieve the broach and retake my seat. It's an attractive bronze flower with glass beads that glows with restrained power. An image forms in my mind of a man with black hair and cruel eyes sneering down at a young woman as she begs him to let her go. She's bruised and protecting her stomach as he hits her again. She is the rightful heir of the fortune he has declared his, but she cannot inherit it until she is claimed by a worthy mate. Their names, Yasmine and Waryn, float around Empy, and the broach rattles. The Emporium has made a decision.

"You may have the broach." I set it down. "However, you are to give Waryn two choices. He either releases you both and gives his daughter everything she is entitled to. Or he accepts the broach and the consequences attached to it."

"You're fucking with me?" Dylan blinks at me, disbelief and hope lightening his aura.

"Nope. Although you will need to change the way the family estate is passed down, Dylan."

"How do you know all this?"

"Same way I knew you were here, what item you wanted, Waryn's name, and that Yasmine is pregnant. Nothing happens in the Emporium without my knowledge."

"She is?" He reaches for the broach but stops short. "Will the consequences harm Yasmine or the baby? Because I'll find another way."

"I admire your resolve." He's changing before our eyes. Fatherhood is rewriting his entire reason and purpose for being alive. It is a glorious sight that I admire greatly.

"Not directly, but depending on the option chosen, she could be shadowed by grief."

"Shadowed by grief, how?"

"That I cannot tell you, but the decision and consequences are not her or your doing." I place the broach in his hand. "I wish you both the best life."

"Is that it?" He grasps the broach to his chest. "I get to leave, alive?"

"In this case, yes. However, if you try anything like this again, it will be the last thing you do." The promise of death is clear and unequivocal.

"Got it." He strides outside, pausing along the way to say, "thanks," before disappearing into the night.

I lower the concealment over the store. Draven and I stare at each other for several long moments. My heart is racing out of my chest, and my legs wouldn't hold me up if my life depended on it, but, despite the crash, I am empowered and where I belong.

"How...?" I flounder, pointing from the sofa to the shelf that housed the broach and door. "It just came to me. I don't get it."

The sputter of necessary information appearing in my mind while we were dealing with Dylan amplifies to a blaring barrage. The room swims, and my entire body shakes. Draven takes my cold hands, but I yank them back to press them against my ears to block out the rush of voices attacking me from every angle. Each one yelling the lessons they have for me.

Nausea rolls through me, and I might be screaming for it to stop; it's hard to tell. I cradle my head, attempting to ward off the agony of more information; my brain is full. I couldn't even list the types of things I now know. I'm suddenly an expert in random subjects no one will ever need again.

"If you look inside yourself, find your connection to Empy." I hear Draven in the grim, dark distance.

"I can't do anything that needs brain power. It's being used." I cry as more items in the Emporium seize the opportunity to bestow me with their history. Adding to the commotion.

"Gather your control and push past it." Draven directs, sending an order directly into my mind, giving me the capacity to see beyond the disorientation and magic. "Examine your core; scrutinize what is there."

Following his authoritative commands, I have the impression of the artifacts, him, and Delly. There's even a hint of many others I've yet to meet. They all have Empy running through them, but each time I come close to properly connecting with the Emporium, it fizzles out, leaving behind another barrage of voices.

"I don't get the store. I feel it around me, as I did Sal's or probably could Paige's, but there's nothing of it in me. It should be, I can tell, but it isn't."

"That's one of the things we need to talk about. The store is kind of broken." He says gently.

"Stop!" I beg as my connection to the store, or rather, the items within its protective fortification, suddenly and painfully explode to life within me. I grab Draven's arm and cling for dear life as my brain quakes within my head, and agony cascades through my body in giant waves.

"She's got it," Draven calls out, and as quickly as it started, it stops. I reach up and touch my face, shocked to find I'm in one piece. I flop back, breathing heavily, and gulp whatever Draven gives me. I think, from the burn, it's bourbon, but I could be wrong.

Gradually, the room comes into focus, and my heart rate slows to something resembling survivable. My hands refuse to stop shaking, and my head throbs like it was crushed and re-inflated a few dozen times.

"That should be a smooth exchange of concepts and insights."

"It wasn't, not at all. I literally thought I was going to be plastered over everything in here." I heave air into my lungs, glad I still can.

"Let's go back to yours. You'll feel better." Draven pulls me to my feet, and I step forward before he can put his arm around me to help.

The house welcomes us with an uplifting reassurance, a safe harbor amongst the chaos and danger. We return to where we were, and our still sparkling wine, as if the last hour didn't happen.

We're both quiet, trying to bring our thoughts to a coherent, un-panicked state.

"The old Merchant does not step down," Draven breaks the silence, "until the new one has served an apprenticeship. Which usually takes between five to ten years. There has never not been a Merchant in place."

"Five to ten years?" I want to bury my head in my hands and pretend this isn't happening. I try really hard to tone the bitterness in my words before I add, "I lack everything needed. Everything."

"No, you don't."

"Double negative makes a positive. That is right, I do lack everything." Draven tries to speak, but I have more to say. "No one told me anything. Not a single thing. I'm not a genius who can guess this stuff. It's all alien to me. I was human with no idea of the essence world until that horrifying announcement. Now I'm supposed to be the Merchant without training. I refuse."

"Then there won't be one, and everything in the store could be claimed by anyone." Draven cocks his head at me, and I give him my best mum look, the one that even works on Ruby. The corner of his mouth curls up a tiny bit. Great, mum-zoned, and he finds me funny. Go, me. "Which would be bad."

"You!" Don't you love an epiphany? "You can do it. You have experience, went to the academy, and were an Overseer. You help your sister in her's."

"Nope." His tone is final, resolute, his face set in stone. "That just isn't possible."

"I don't see why not. It's perfect." Relief and loss float through me in equal measure. "The store needs you more than it needs me."

"It's not a store." Draven shakes his head, swallowing.

"Store, Emporium, it's the same thing."

"It is really a depository for objects of the arcane and non-light magic to be held and protected."

A twitchy, indiscriminate sensation sweeps up my spine, leaving goosebumps in its wake.

"Only to be released to the worthy, who provide justification and compensation." The words stream from deep within me, from the knowledge that I still can not fully access, even though it nearly killed me.

"That's right. Who decides who is justified and what the compensations should be?" Draven's gaze bores into me.

"They either are or are not justified, and the compensation is dependent on the justification." A fresh warning hits me square in the chest, knocking the air from my lungs. "Unworthy people who cannot justify their desire for an object are on their way and must be stopped."

I get a vision of a woman with knee-length raven hair and cruel iridescent eyes standing at the bow of a boat sailing towards the island. The ornately engraved silver sword hanging from her waist has ended too many lives for her to turn back now. She turns to an emaciated, bruised man, chained to the helm and clicks her fingers. He quakes and trembles until she snaps them again. He corrects the trajectory of their journey, and she turns away.

The shroud of evil soars around them, masking their presence and location. She will not be deterred easily.

This goes straight to another vision of a woman wearing a long, hooded cloak arriving on the island, carrying an urn and purple book. She collapses on the ground where the Emporium is, claws it with her bare hands, throws something into the hole, and covers it. She kneels over the freshly dug earth, her shoulders shaking as she cradles the urn close. Finally, when she's in the last moments of her life, she writes in the book. I see the words, but they mean nothing to me, characters I can't even place as being similar to any current language. She closes the book, lies down, clutching it to her chest, and casts her lifeless gaze skywards.

Staring at my face on the dying woman shocks me. I bolt up and out the door, heaving breaths and desperately trying to get my inner turmoil under some kind of control. Strong arms wrap around me, encapsulating me in safety, stability and...there should be more, something from within him, but I can't sense what. There's nothing from Draven except a fragmented bond to something he yearns to cling onto.

Draven holds me at arm's length, searching my face.

"There's a woman with knee-length black hair on her way. She's killed and will again." I can't tell him about the woman with my face or the book, but that vision is the key, the explanation for everything.

"We'll stop her together." He promises.

"Draven, how long has the island been inhabited for?" No human, essence, or otherwise, had set foot on it before her.

"Many, many thousands of years. The town hall has an archive with more history, and I think the library. Why?"

"Doesn't matter. They're getting closer. I need my suit from Sera." I mentally order the house to lock itself down, which should prevent someone from using it to gain access to the Emporium. I search inside me for the same type of connection to Empy, but it just isn't there. Instead, all I find is a void that weeps to be filled.

Draven catches my arm and tugs me around to face him.

"For what it's worth, I'll be by your side doing all I can. But I'm not sure I'll be much good." His intense, concerned gaze leaves mine for a moment, and a world of pain shines in his eyes when he looks back at me. His voice drops to a tortured whisper. "I could explain, but we don't have time."

"You are not broken, Draven." I stroke his cheek, wishing I could make him see himself as others do. "I promise you."

Fifteen

Sera ushers us inside her store, passes me a pile of black and purple leather garments, and shoves me into a dressing room.

I strip and fold my clothes for later. The leather trousers fit like a glove. The thick, dark purple leather has several black leather panels going down the side, giving a smidgeon of ventilation. Leather and tropical weather do not mix, especially for a perimenopause woman who can't really cope with the heat to begin with.

The top clings like nothing I would ever even consider wearing. My breasts are encased in a built-in bra, and I have to confess they look damn perky. The high neck and long sleeves cover all the way to the back of my hands.

This is something my sister would wear for a photoshoot or acting part. It couldn't be more modern superhero if it had a letter printed on the front and a cape flapping about behind.

"How's it going?" Sera calls.

"Fine." I twist in the cubicle to see how my backside looks. If I have to run around wearing a second skin, there will be no chocolate anything. The curtain swishes open, and Sera yanks me out. Several women crowd me, poking and prodding, making last-minute stitches with giant needles. I stand motionless, letting them do their thing.

"These as well." I'm passed a pair of heavy boots that will kill my feet. I slide them on, and they convert before my eyes into, I wouldn't stay stylish but less ready to work on the building site. My feet cry out in joy at their perfect arch support.

"Now we just need to check it'll retract." Someone says, placing a bracelet on my wrist and tapping the decorative purple flower. My clothes, everything except panties, vanish, leaving me desperate to cover up.

"That won't give you much protection," Draven sighs behind me. I spin around because him seeing my nearly bare backside apparently isn't enough for me. Thoughts die in my head, and my mouth goes dry because my cutie has been transformed into a deadly warrior. His black leather trousers cling, and I cannot wait to see his bottom in them. The shirt molds to the contours of his chest, emphasizing his delectable frame and height.

"Tap the flower." Sera nudges me. I do, and my suit is back. Sucking in all my lumps and bumps, saving me from having to hold my stomach in any longer. "You are to keep the bracelet on at all times. The outfit will appear over whatever you have on as if they weren't there. You won't need to strip in the future." She tells me. "There are no weapons worked into it yet, please bear that in mind. Same for yours, Draven."

"Thanks, appreciate it," Draven calls over his shoulder, dragging me outside toward the encroaching danger.

᧞ ᧞ ᧞ ᧞

Dusk is falling as we head back to the Emporium. Draven attaches the sword he had earlier to his back and places several other items in his pockets. His bracelet has a blue dragon, very similar to his.

"Let's see what we can find for you. Can you shoot a gun?" I shake my head. "Can you throw straight?" I shrug an ish motion, and Draven grunts.

"I can hit quite hard." I ignore his wince because if Raven, as I'm calling her, is close enough for me to punch, she'll have killed me with her sword. I run my hand over the line of weapons, waiting for something to feel as if it belongs to me. None do.

Until I'm wrenched to a long, silver chain hanging on the wall. The leather-bound handle secures itself in my grasp, sending instructions on how to use it.

A quick test shot ties Draven's hands together and a small tug brings him to within kissing distance. Hmm, interrogation distance.

"Impressive." A flick of my wrist, and he's released. He smirks at me with heat pouring from his eyes. "No getting any ideas. That's my role."

It takes me a moment to think what he means, and, I swear, every inch of my skin is bright red with embarrassment.

I wind the chain up, and attach it to a loop on my trousers, urging my thoughts past the image of Draven restrained and at my mercy or vice versa.

A sudden foreboding swoops through my core, bolstering my obligation to being the Merchant. That's not how I should feel. It should be a partnership, a coming together to create one whole. For now, I can only make the best of what I have or die trying. Possibly literally.

"Stay behind me as much as possible. I'll protect you, I promise." Draven vows.

"We will stand united. Equals. Where one of us has the experience, muscle, and stamina, and I have a chain." I shrug, twisting my lips. "That was supposed to be a lot more motivational."

"We'll have all the motivation we handle." Draven places a long, thin sword on my back, which melts into my suit, and straps a knife to my thigh.

"I look like a badass," I say, getting a gander of the shapely woman as I pass in front of a cracked mirror.

"You are a badass." His gaze roams my body, making me feel like more than just a badass.

"Let's go defend this place." I'm not going to lie; my legs are shaking, my heart beats are shoving so much adrenaline around my system, I may use a lifetime's supply before Raven arrives.

The street is deserted. Considering people have no idea exactly what the Emporium is, they do know when to keep out of the way.

The steady thrum of approaching danger beats through me and into the air. I try one last time to tune into Empy, but the interference is not only louder but underlined with a scurry of bitterness. It's a distraction I can't afford, so with regret and nothing more than the hope I can open it later, I slam the connection shut.

Draven and I stand shoulder to shoulder, or more like head to chest. These boots add some height but not that much.

The saltwater scent of the sea blends with the stench of suspense and nearing malevolence.

Draven's steady breathing gives me something to ground my frantically unraveling thoughts and swirling inner emotions.

The shadowed figure of Raven strides purposely towards us, dragging another by the hair.

"A welcome committee?" She drawls, her accent a mix, possibly South American and Greek. Her sword catches the light as she holds it ready. "How bothersome."

"Let him go." I stand tall and speak from the gut. She smirks, and the sharp sound of his head hitting the stone ground echoes down the street. Almost calling me to flee after it. "Put your sword away."

"After you and your pet." Her eyes rake over Draven, focusing on parts she has no reason to. He stiffens beside me, a slight but menacing growl falling from his lips. Her scrutiny targets me, and no inch is left unexamined, evaluated, and found wanting. "Dragon, they are the best leather. But who am I telling."

A muscle in Draven's jaw ticks, and my fingertips brush my trousers. Please do not let the unusually thick and supple leather be from a dragon.

"Step aside, little girl. I have things to do and tiresome conversations with a *genie* is not part of my plan." The disgust she packs into genie ignites a pride I didn't know I had in being one and my anger.

She yanks the man up by his hair and continues toward us, sighing when we don't move.

"Go away." Draven growls, his lips pulled tight over his teeth and muscles flexing.

"You two are starting to really piss me off. Now go forth and multiply before I render you nothing but a pile of body parts." She drops the man again and draws a second, thicker sword, pointing both at us with the expertise you see in movies.

Draven retrieves his from his back and matches her stance. I ready my chain, and sinister spikes extend from the links.

"If you've hurt Valeria, those body parts will be reanimated and tortured time and time again." She steps closer, running the tip of her engraved sword down my cheek. I give her a what-the-hell look and take a half step back.

"What do you mean? If we've hurt her?" I point at her, throwing her into a world of confusion. "Why would we hurt her?"

I knock her sword away with a finger and thrust my hands on my hips. "Well?"

Draven is nearly behind her with his knife poised to her throat when she twirls around, attacking. The clang of metal is as terrifying as it is exhilarating. They parry; it is a parry with swords, isn't it? Then stare at each other with cocked heads and bemused expressions.

"I detest destroying my entertainment, but let me introduce you." The sardonic, civilized voice of the vampire who was with my Adonis cuts through us. "Merchant, Procurer, and what title do you prefer in these modern times, Raven?"

It's the first time my nickname has been used as her actual name.

"Titles are outdated. You can not be the Merchant." If Raven found me wanting before, now I'm something she needs to scrape from her shoe. "Where is Valeria?"

"That is a *QI* question mark card." The newcomer dramatically waves his arms and bows. The frilled sleeves of his emerald green velvet jacket accentuates the movement. We stare at him, unimpressed. "It means..."

"We all know what it means. We watch the show, everyone watches the show." Raven snaps, gripping her sword tightly and shaking it at him in small, stabbing motions.

"I don't." Draven does one of those shoulders-to-the-ears shrugs. I can't help but chuckle, much to his annoyance.

"Poor boy, you need to watch more TV." The vampire pats his shoulder, laying on the sympathy. Draven quirks a brow at him, flexing his neck like someone spoiling for a fight.

"Behave, you two. You are meant to be adults, not horny teens vying for the head cheerleader." Raven huffs. They step back sharply, not breaking eye contact.

Raven is not a threat. She's a... possibly friend, it's hard to tell, but at the moment, she is not here for nefarious reasons. I have never been so glad to be wrong.

"Who is that?" The vampire kicks the lifeless form lying on the ground with the tip of his shiny, leather loafer.

"One of the horde on their way to invade the island." Raven tells him as if that's nothing. "Nice to meet you, bye."

"Wait, you can't go!" I dart to catch her arm.

"Why? Any Merchant could handle his crew." She tugs free and strides away again. Tears prick my eyes. I'm not sure how much roller coaster-ing of safe and in mortal danger I can cope with in this short amount of time.

The vampire calls, checking the man's pulse. "You could have left him alive. Raven, there's something you may need to know."

"Get your own snacks." She stares down at me then at Draven. "I'm not going to like this, am I?"

I shake my head and trudge back to the Emporium, tapping my bracelet before remembering I'm practically naked under it. I smack it quickly but not before the vampire gets an eyeful of the glory that is my nearly nude front and Raven my backside.

"I'm still getting used to everything." I shudder as embarrassment courses through my midlife veins.

"Take your time." The vampire slowly raises his amused but appreciative gaze to mine. Draven's hand lands on my lower back, propelling me inside to my chair. He stands by my side like a sentry guard.

"I remember you." Raven takes the other chair, talking to Draven. "Valeria had high hopes for you. You abandoned her for the academy."

"I didn't abandon anyone. I went to the academy." He grinds out through clenched teeth.

"Now he's back, and no one knows why. It's very mysterious and not the least bit concerning." The vampire informs Raven with a mocking, serious expression.

"Stop making trouble for everyone. It'll bite you on the ass." Raven rolls her eyes at him. "What is going on here?"

There's a small pause as I decide how to word my thoughts while everyone eyes me.

"You're struggling to tune into the Emporium, aren't you?" I can feel her probing and Empy's hesitance.

"That you can sense that means you are attached to it, but everything is wrong." She stands and walks over to Percy, lifting his thimble, and then handles a few other items.

"Trying to find your next item to auction off to whoever wants it, my dear?" The vampire's taunting tone grates what's left of my nerves and tolerance.

"Who are you, and what is your part in this?" I ask him, not enjoying how his gaze drops to my breasts before he focuses on my face. A puff of smoke floats from Draven.

"I am Kedar, I have been on Whispering longer than most anyone, even before the Emporium. I know every living and not so living soul who sets foot on its welcoming shores." He sits back, resting an ankle on his knee, and straightens a diamond-encrusted cufflink.

"But do you have a reason for being here, right this second?" I regard Kedar carefully, he arrived just in the knick of time, as if he was watching and waiting to see how it would go.

"Well, I did prevent you from attempting to harm someone who, on this occasion, came to aid the Merchant." He meets my gaze, not quite challenging, more assessing me right back.

"Do you always do that? Make people look both good and bad?" It's petty, but I long to mess up his impeccable hair and crease his silk tie. He merely winks at me.

"You'll get used to him." Raven wanders past us to the cast iron cupboard on the far side and runs her hand down it. "The protection is still as strong, which is good, but odd."

"Why odd?"

Raven returns to her seat. Her elegance and poise do not conceal how deadly she is but add to her enigma.

"Because the Emporiums is in disarray, which should weaken its ability to maintain such things. Is this related to The Adjustment?" The last bit is aimed very directly at Draven, who swallows and remains staring straight ahead.

"That would be an affirmative." Kedar almost loses his smirk for a hint of genuine interest.

"We should worry more about the imminent danger." Draven breaks his silence as Empy shoots a warning through me.

"Thirty bobcat shifters. It'll be a mildly entertaining evening. We won't even break a sweat." Raven dismisses. "I'll have to tap my sources for more information on The Adjustment. Where is Valeria? It isn't like her to miss the fun."

"She went traveling." Kedar turns to me, cocking his head. "See, I didn't mention how she left everyone high and dry or how she failed to secure Empy."

"One day, Kedar, someone will stick a big old, silver knife in your back." Raven sighs at him.

"They're here. They've landed on the island." I gulp and clench my hands together.

"Is this your first rodeo?" I do a Draven and remain silent, and it's as effective as it was for him. Kedar's grin spreads over his entire face, replacing the sardonic sneer. "Oh, I do like to help a lady with her firsts."

"Ewww, creepoid much." Sera recoils from the door, looking seriously hot in skin-tight, dark red leather trousers and bustier, carrying a long, thick, golden sword and jacket. Kedar's mouth hangs open.

"When did you grow up?" He clears his throat to cover up his squeaky voice.

"Thought you were the expert on all things Whispering." Draven throws over this shoulder as we exit the Emporium.

"Valeria trained me. I can fight." Sera assures us all. Placing my folded clothes from earlier on the counter.

"No one trained me," I creak, forcing myself to admit it.

"No one has trained you?" Raven cuts in, horror rolling off her in great tidal waves. I shake my head. "That will need to be rectified. For now, stay behind us."

"Don't get distracted by the view." Kedar winks, wiggling his lean hips from side to side. His clothing transforms into a three-piece, black leather suit with a slight blue hue. It even has ruffled sleeves and a collar.

Feeling helpless is the pits. That sense of uselessness never fails to provoke each and every deep-seated insecurity I have.

A GENIE'S NEW START

As I follow everyone outside, listening to their orders about how and where to hide if needed, it plunders the depths of my being. Filling the void that should be swamped with the love of my mother and daughter. The self-assurance of a marriage that ended in some decent way. Even the resolve of having a direction in life.

None of that resides inside me. I'm nothing more than a scared and helpless little girl who is nothing but a liability. It's a bitter pill to swallow and a major setback to claiming my new start.

As much as I vow to put that right and learn all the skills I need, it doesn't help me or the people standing before me ready to do battle and possibly die.

Draven turns, his armor of ruthless savagery is lifted only by the tenderness gleaming from his eyes. He lifts my chin with his finger, seeing into my core and everything I keep hidden.

"You're doing great. Most people would have run a mile." He indicates behind him. "Remember, we've been doing this for years and years."

I'm about to argue and make him see that I'm just not good enough, I'm already failing at the first hurdle, when he gently kisses my forehead, stealing my negative emotions and self-condemning thoughts.

"We've got dance partners," Kedar announces as a hoard of caterwauling men run at us with swords, knives, and clubs raised.

The clash of metal on metal followed by screams is sickening, but it's how quickly the men perish that really turns my stomach. Most are in no better state than the man Raven dragged in.

Draven fights with brutal effectiveness, remorselessly going for the kill from the outset. Within moments, he's taken out three men. Kedar's theatrical style could not be more different, although it is just as effective. He swings his sword with flourishing movements, jumping high in the air to land behind his opponents before he ends their suffering.

Raven is possibly the most impressive. She's precise, contained, and lethally efficient. I adore how she stays close to Sera, protecting but letting her do her thing. While Sera is good, she lacks the fluidity of the other three. I'm in awe of them all.

The chain on my hip vibrates, calling me. I clench it, breathing through my self-loathing. My hand lifts, wrist flicks, and the chain wraps around the neck of a weedy little man sneaking behind Kedar. I yank it with everything I have just as his silver knife breaches the skin covering Kedar's carotid artery. Kedar leaps back and winks at me with a low bow, rising to slide his sword into a man's gut.

I didn't think we'd lose, but seeing us winning is a life-affirming moment, and I helped. I did my, albeit small, part. My gasp of awakening boldness is obliterated by a gunshot and Sera's guttural curse of agony.

White hot fury hijacks my reactions. My hand twirls, and my fingers click. The gun rises into the air, turns, and fires at the man who was holding it. I stumble backward, staring at my hand, my silent, traumatized scream overwhelming the waning battle.

Unseen by anyone but me, a dying cat shifter pulls another gun and aims it at Draven. I watch my hand in terror as it again twirls, and the gun twists. My fingers click, and he shoots himself instead.

Paralyzed by my inability to process what I've seen and done, I crumble to the ground, draw my knees to my chest, and hug them tightly, desperately trying to drag air into my burning, constricted lungs. Tears stream down my cheeks.

"Hey, it's over. Let's get you inside." Sera cajoles, gently stroking my back. She and Raven drag me to my feet and half carry me to Empy. I turn to check Draven and Kedar, seeing them piling bodies into a heap. "Don't worry about that."

"But the bodies." I manage through my raspy throat.

"Will be taken care of," Raven says crisply.

"But how?"

"Draven is a dragon, honey." I gape at Sera, catching Draven shifting and hovering a few feet above the gruesome mass of the perished. Small, almost harmless flames meander from his mouth, and I realize how they'll be taken care of. I wrap my arms around my middle, wondering if I'll ever feel anything but icy numbness.

I'm sent into the kitchen to put my normal clothes back on, followed by my leather suit. That way, I'll have it whenever I need it. I do it quickly before I can contemplate and tap the bracelet to make the leather reminder disappear from view.

I collapse onto my chair seconds before my legs give out. Sera drapes a blanket over my shoulders and presses a hot cup of tea into my hands. I stare at the steam rising from my brew, seeing the faces of the men who are longer alive because of me. I clicked my fingers, and they shot themselves; I didn't wish or even think it, but it happened, anyway.

"Drink; it'll do you good." Sera rubs my leg, lifting my mug. I comply, and it burns with more than heat. "I added fae whiskey, so no slugging it from the bottle."

She's part fae and wizard, something about that stays out of my reach, and I gulp my drink without questioning what properties she infused. Within moments of setting my empty cup down, my insides are warm, and my heart rate starts to decrease. Draven walks in and crouches before me. Kedar hangs back by the door.

"You okay?" I nod. I wasn't hurt. They kept me safe. He grows more intense, his eyes the lightest shade of gray, shimmering with an intensity that compels me to be truthful. "Really?"

"I killed... twice," I whisper because verbalizing it will make it more real.

"You did." He encases my hands in his and places them on his chest. "Thank you for saving my life. You were amazing."

"I killed." My tortured whimper is painful even to my own ears. "Murdered."

"It wasn't murder, but we'll talk about that more tomorrow. I'm taking you home." He lifts me as he stands as if I weigh nothing and tucks me against him, wrapping me in protection and security. "Could you meet us for breakfast?"

I tune out the arrangements, knowing Draven is doing his best for me. He carries me bridal style through the back of the Emporium, the secret gate, and into my house. Our wine sits on the table, undrunk and unwanted.

"Ginny, I'm not leaving you alone. We can sleep in your bed..."

"No! I don't want to be straight." I was standing upright when I clicked my fingers, and the fear it'll happen again is taking over my mind.

"Okay, chair it is." Draven sits us in an overstuffed chair, wraps us in a blanket and reclines it enough to be almost comfy but still letting me feel like I'm sitting. "Get some sleep. It's been a long day."

My eyes will not close. For an eternity, I can only stare sightlessly ahead, focusing only on Draven's heartbeat under my cheek.

Sixteen

The fresh day starts far too early. My sleep was disturbed with dreams of me clicking my fingers and wiping out half the galaxy. Suddenly, that plotline in *Marvel* doesn't feel so impossible.

I ease from Draven's arms. Even asleep, he's still a fierce warrior. It does nothing to soothe his harsh features. After a quick shower, I dress in practical shorts and a vest top with a long blouse ready to throw on for the ceremony. As much as I'd love to curl into a ball and lament how I took two lives, I have responsibilities and people depending on me. I pull my hair into a messy bun and add a touch of makeup to hide my dark bags.

I make it downstairs as Draven's long lashes flicker open. His initial confusion clears to concern. He prowls towards me, his steely gaze searching every inch of my face before zeroing in on my eyes.

"I'm fine and have a busy day. Do you want coffee?" I stride past him, flick the kettle on, and inspect the pantry. "I have pastries for breakfast."

"Ginny, we need to talk about yesterday." He tells me cautiously.

"Maybe, maybe not. What is there to say?" He growls softly, and I carry on. "Today is about Sal and his store. That's where I'll be."

"Sera, Raven, and..."

"Will wait or not, but not today." I shove a pastry into my mouth and make my tea. Checking the time, I realize it's later than I'd like. "I have to go. Thanks for last night."

Guilt trickles through me as I hop onto a scooter to take the long way to Sal's store to avoid any reminders of last night. There are worse things than allowing myself a few hours to deny anything happened.

Seeing the frustration across Sal's face as he tries to enter his store is a shock, not only because it means the store is not happy, but also because his features are clear. The shroud of darkness that cloaked his appearance has gone completely. He's a man with loss and hope flowing through his aura.

"What's going on?"

"I want to paint the door black." Sal huffs. "The store disagrees."

"Then we'll table that for later." I stroke the dark blue door and tune into the store. There's a sense of doomful inevitability and mourning. I can't help but sympathize. There is a comparability to our situations. Our purpose has changed, and our existences have taken new paths we didn't choose and could never have predicted. We're both scrambling to catch up and survive the tumultuous transformations that have been thrust upon us. This is not natural evolution or something we wanted.

The door creaks open, and I enter. The final piece of art remains illuminated by a new wall lamp shining from above it. The store's single, lingering token of what will always be its true purpose.

I stand before the landscape painting, drinking in the tranquil scene and bright, cheery colors and let myself get lost in the beautiful, delicate flowers and crisp mountain air. Acknowledging to this store and myself that we can pursue our new directions or fade away with the old. Neither is ideal, but they are the only routes open to us.

I stand back next to Sal as people filter past, all silently taking a moment of meditative reflection with the painting. Their emotions charge the air with a heady mix of sentiments. I follow the last person out, allowing Sal his own introspection.

He comes outside, closes the door, turns his back to the store, and dips his head. We all do the same. Waiting to discover if the store will find the strength to survive and thrive is nerve-wrack-ing. I clasp my hands together, drag air into my lungs and push it out, not permitting my thoughts to move past this moment.

Sal lifts his head, his shoulders tense, and turns back. "Yes!"

I spin around to see tables, chairs, bookshelves, and a huge noticeboard. The black door glides open as Sal approaches. He puts his hand flat on the doorframe, taking a deep breath, and over the threshold.

"I would like to welcome you all to Whispering's new Educations Center." Sal bellows, and we all cheer. "Paige, we need us some books."

"Thank crap." She calls, linking her arms through mine, and Sera's yanking us away. She checks over her shoulder. "What the hell happened last night, and if you say nothing, I'll never talk to either of you again."

"Paige, don't ask questions you shouldn't have the answer to." Sera hisses, her head darting to peer behind us.

"Ginny, you're shaking like one of my kids when they've been caught eating bugs in the yard." Paige yanks me into her store, slams the door, and waves her hands around. "Right, now no one can hear. Sera, why is Ginny shaking?"

"Paige, leave her be and let it all alone." Sera insists, walking around the shelves. "Which of the many book mountains do we take?"

Within a few moments, Paige has numerous piles of books stacked up outside her store. Several helpers meander over to collect them.

"Was Draven involved?" Paige continues, fury simmering around her like a volcano ready to erupt.

"He helped. He was on the right side." Sera says softly, patting her arm. Paige deflates and nods quickly.

What the hell! Was there a chance he might not have been?

"Let's get back." Sera shepherds us outside, and I'm left to trail behind Sera and Paige, who looks like she'd lost about a thousand pounds of baggage weighing her shoulders down. The rest of the day passes in a blur of questions, suggestions, and the faces of the men I killed drifting through my psyche.

As the sun starts to lose some of the searing heat, the Learning Center nears completion, leaving me gaping at a teaching kitchen that, a few hours before, was solid ground, as in under the store. Below that is a multipurpose space with tools, desks, and science equipment. I gave up asking how ages ago, I was getting too many odd looks.

A whiteboard with a list of classes has pride of place by the door. The variety of things being taught is mind-boggling. Everything from art to Latin. I've been roped in to teach about life in the UK. I'm debating on simply handing out umbrellas and randomly tipping buckets of water over them.

"You did very well." Gran stands beside me, wiping a speck of dust off a countertop. "It never ceases to amaze me what Whispering is capable of. Or you."

Gran's calculating stare sends a wave of caution through my fatigue, scraping at a memory in the very recesses of my mind.

"It's been a long day. I'm ready for a shower. Thanks for helping." I hightail it away before her all-too-assessing eyes delve too deeply.

"Ginny," Sal grabs me into a big bear hug, lifting me from the ground. I adore seeing his smile and optimism. It's infectious. He's even more of a gentle giant than I anticipated. He's literally grown a foot up and across during the day, making him a physically imposing man, but his caring nature shines in every cell of his enormous body. "I can't thank you enough."

"You already did." I half laugh and half scream as he twirls me through the air.

"Next Wednesday, when the store holders get together, I'll bring the food, wine, and beer." He sets me on my feet, and I hold the counter as my brain catches on that I'm no longer hurtling around in a circle.

"Sounds good." The Learning Center sighs and relaxes further. I stroke the careworn wood beneath my palm in gratitude, relief, and acknowledgment. It could have gone either way, and the prospect of losing this precious space is heartbreaking. "I'm going home. Don't be here all night. You open early tomorrow."

"Ahh, the early birds' cooking class." He grins with pure joy, despite the shadow of loss still clinging to him.

"That's the one." He gives me another hug before I stroll away with a sense of accomplishment burning bright within me. It's second only to giving birth to the twins.

Each step from the Learning Center and closer to Empy drags my mood down until I'm standing before Empy with my inner swirling callously tormenting and shaming me. The glass is warm and comforting as I trace the pattern of the ornate window.

I'm no nearer to understanding if this is the future I'm meant to claim or if I've got caught up with something that has nothing to do with me. The sedative lure of the Pacific is too much to resist, and I carry on to the cliff face's sheer drop at the southwestern edge of Whispering.

The menacing waves crash against the rocks at total odds with the calm, sparkling water just a few hundred feet out. I cautiously peer over the edge, it goes on forever. Testing a theory, I drop a stone and count until it hits the waves. About halfway, it vanishes. It wasn't a tiny pebble but a substantial and heavy rock. It proves magic is manipulating the area. I cannot be sure whether the phenomenon is merely an illusion or if someone would be smashed to pieces if they tried to land here.

Glorious, tranquil solitude wraps around me. This is what I've yearned for all day. Draven has not strayed far from my side. Neither did Sera or Raven. One of them was everywhere I looked. Their support is a force to be reckoned with, even for me.

I rest my weary legs on a boulder that's shockingly comfortable under my backside. After a solid nine hours of being on my feet, they ache a lot. My knees aren't everything they used to be, either. Forty may be the new twenty, but no one tells your joints.

As hunger ransacks my stomach, I decide it's time to hobble home, eat, and flake out for the evening with a movie or, better still, a good book. I trudge away, debating my to-be-read list. The next read is a big decision, monumental, really.

From nowhere, long, thick, sharp claws wrap around me, trapping my arms against my body, and I'm snatched into the air and out to sea. I scream my best and loudest, but not even I can hear it. I thrash and struggle to escape, kicking to make contact with a leg and hurl my head back, hoping to knock the air from my kidnapper's lungs.

"You want me to let you go?" A freakishly disembodied and sinister voice scoffs.

"Yes, you... argh." As suddenly as I was seized, I'm dropped and hurtling toward the deep water of the Pacific Ocean. My chances of swimming all the way back to shore are about as good as my chances of flying. So, naturally, I flap my arms as if they're going to sprout into wings and let me peacefully glide to dry land.

I hit the ocean with a thwack and sink, swallowing copious amounts of salty water. Panic assaults me; my attempts to swim only see me descending deeper, fish swim past and, holy crap, I swear there's a hungry shark eyeing me for dinner.

My lungs are on fire, my eyes bulge, and my limbs are in agony. My body's demand to breathe strengthens the dread and crushes my efforts to rise to the surface. Exterminating my hope of survival.

Large dark spots float through my vision, accompanied by images from my life. My final memory as I succumb to the darkness is playing cards with the twins after Christmas dinner.

Seventeen

I come to coughing and spluttering, retching copious quantities of salty seawater. Instinct makes me expel as much of it as I can. The risk of drowning does not end merely because you're out of the water.

"That will teach you to do as I say." Shiny, pointed black boots step into the edges of my vision. I don't bother lifting my head to see who they belong to; that takes energy, and I have none.

"You didn't say anything." I wheeze, reminding myself I'm not in the water, and oxygen is all around me again.

"You will pay for what you did. He was a good man." My gaze shoots up to eyes that make my blood run cold. I believed seeing the lifeless stares of the men who died at my hands whenever I closed my eyes was their revenge, but it seems they left someone behind.

These eyes, ones filled with anger, revenge, and grief, belong to a young girl, I'm guessing mid teens, with long caramel-brown hair, wearing a Xena Warrior Princess style outfit that exposes an unreasonable amount of flesh. She carries a spear that towers over her tiny frame and glistens in the dazzling sunlight.

I pull myself up to a chair and reach forward to a glass of clear liquid on the table. Not caring it's half drunk.

"What the hell is this?" The warm fluid has a gone-off fruity taste that curdles my stomach.

"No idea. It was on the boat when I stole it." She sits opposite, crossing one leg over the other, practically showing me what she had for breakfast.

"So, what now?" Whispering is a dot in the distance, and she has enough weapons strapped to her body for me to be dead before I can unleash my chain. The wooden ship isn't much more than four seats around a table, an odd yet practical design for someone who wants to bob about close to the shore. I would not want to trust it on the open sea.

"You die to avenge him." Her voice cracks, and her hand clenches around a long, thin knife on her thigh.

"Do I get to find out why he and his cronies were invading Whispering first?" It's been troubling me that we never found that out.

"He would never do such a thing!" She swings the spear, poising it inches from my chest. I shove it aside, taking in her youth, disbelief, and sense of righteous anger.

"Sorry to disappoint you, but that's exactly what they did. What was he to you, father?" Her eyes harden to a little girl's. "Uncle? Grandfather?"

The mother part of me wants to scold her for dabbling in matters she knows nothing about. The rest of me is busy debating how to survive.

"He was my everything. He raised me, trained me, and loved me." Her chin rises defiantly, her bottom lip protruding and quivering.

"Now he's left you alone to fend for yourself in an outfit that makes you look like a... stripper. You should be in school with clothes that cover your tushie and a proper bed to sleep in."

Her breath hitches, and she whimpers but regains her composure with the practiced speed of someone who has never been considered or cared for. She's been dragged along and treated as a possession.

"You hungry?" She does her best not to nod. "Do you have anything worthwhile to your name?"

"I have family honor that will see you dead." She sits up, straightening her spine, her sea-green eyes sparkling with fear.

"No, it won't. Get your stuff together. You're staying with me tonight, and we'll sort the future tomorrow." She pauses, half standing.

"Why?"

"Because I'm hungry, tired ,and done with this. You need a bed and meal, and for the love of chocolate, put some clothes on." I snap at her, forcibly ignoring how her chest spills from the corset.

"I don't have anything else to wear."

"We'll get you something." I reach into my pocket for my phone to message Sera for a few outfits for her and curse when it's gone.

"I'll fetch it." She jumps overboard in a perfect dive and disappears below the waves. I flop back, closing my eyes. I might have dozed off because I jump out of my skin when water drips on my face when she leaps onto the boat.

"You're still here." She gives me a small, watery smile, passing me my phone.

"Indeed." I message Sera, guessing my companion's size. She replies instantly, asking me where the (we'll say flicking) hell I am. I assure her I'm fine and shove my phone away.

"Why?" Her uncertainty wars with her cynicism, further yanking my mummy heartstrings.

"I came here to claim a new future, and it looks like you need the same. Do you?" I fix her with my most intimidating stare, sapping the reserve of energy I'm running on.

"Does it involve stealing?"

"No!" My hands land palms down on the glass tabletop. "Nothing illegal."

"Then I'm in." Her grin highlights how slightly child-like her face is.

"Tomorrow, we need to sit down and have a long conversation, but, for now, what's your name?"

"Bertha," her sullen shoulders and sulk says it all.

"New future, new name." I shrug, hating Bertha as well. I'm sure it suits some people, but not her. Her mouth opens and closes, fretting as the first letter of some or other name fails to spring forward. "Think about it; for now, I'll call you Bee."

Something in her lights up, but she moves to the helm before I break through the grogginess of nearly dying and inviting my would-be murderer into my home.

We sail back with only the sound of the ocean and engine breaking the silence. The wind and sun dries out my hair to a crinkle, which will take a long soak in conditioner and a deep oil treatment to sort out. Bee guides the boat into a dock where an angry, short, fat man with a superiority complex rants to a tall, dark, handsome specimen in a sheriff's uniform. Complete with khaki shorts showcasing his muscular legs.

Bee quakes as the sheriff's narrowed eyes lock on her, his inviting lips thinned into a grim line.

"Bee, I think we might have taken the wrong boat for a test run." I drag her out past the men, nodding to them. "My bad, and apologies, gentleman."

We get to the scooter stand; I check out two and zoom away at full speed with Bee on my tail. If you're picturing a fast, exciting escape, I hate to burst your bubble, but electric scooters are not sports cars. It takes yonks before the sheriff's steely gaze no longer sends goosebumps spiking from my skin.

We're at Sera's store before I fully look over my shoulder, expecting to see my hunk, aka the sheriff, right behind me. Humor and determination splinting over his chiseled features, handcuffs ready in his big, powerful hands. I shake off my screaming libido and push Bee into a changing room with a few age-appropriate outfits.

"Who the hell is she, and where have you been? Draven and Raven are beside themselves." Sera hisses with equal concern and anger, right into my ear.

"Hey, their names rhyme. How did I not notice?" I take in Sera's glower and hand poised over her leather bracelet and give the mother of all sighs. "I'm okay, unhurt, and here. She's a scared child who is alone in the world."

"She should go to the GC." Sera crosses her arms over her chest, hands pulled into tight fists. I wrack my brain, trying to recall what it stands for. "GC is the Guidance Committee. They look after essence people who have nowhere to go and so on."

"She does have somewhere. Mine." I match Sera's stance. Bee steps from the changing room in a flouncy, bright pink dress with lace frills, frantic alarm sprinting from her at breakneck speed. She lifts the floppy bow around the neck and shakes her head.

"Please, no." Bee twitches and fidgets. I can't blame her. The vulgar star-shaped buttons alone are a violation to good taste.

"Crap, I gave you the wrong stuff." Sera twists and hurls another pile of clothes at Bee. "Quick, you cannot be seen in that."

"You think?" Bee rolls her eyes, drawing the curtain behind her. Within seconds, the dress is shoved out.

"Who is that for?" I watch her put it on a hanger, cringing as I can feel the crackle of the fabric abrade my skin.

"One of the vampires." Sera swallows, checking through the door. "See how the frills give a stunning, innocent, girly look?"

"Yeah." Sensing Sera has a reason for this. They've been starched to the point they could cut through glass. Innocent is not how I would describe the dress. Sinisterly warped and depraved are much more apt. But I have a suit made from dragon hide. Dragons are shifters, meaning I'm wearing a person's skin. I lost my privilege to judge.

Bee steps out in knee-length, dark blue jean shorts, a black vest top, and denim tennis shoes. Dimming the untamed qualities of her harsh attitude.

"It fits. We'll take it all." The other items are bagged up and passed to Bee to lug around. "I'm starving. Who's up for dinner?"

Sera sees Bee salivate and drops a smidgeon of her animosity toward the girl.

"There's a great BBQ place in Main Town that always has tables. I'll lead the way." Sera locks the store and quietly says a few words to the door I don't catch. Bee bows her head before reverently stroking the thick wood.

Stanley's BBQ and BBQ, one day I'll ask why it's repeated, but not today. It's busy, loud, and smells like bliss had a delicious love child with every aromatic spice on the planet. The menu is thicker than some novels I've read. Bee and I stare at it, then at each other, our mouths hanging slightly open. Possibly drooling.

"Lay it outs, "wave your hand over it and ask for a dinner option."

"Do we become dinner?" Bee holds the menu between her thumb and finger, ready to lob it across the room. Sera shakes her head bemusedly.

"Like this." Raven appears nearly out of nowhere in a black leather outfit fit for Catwoman, her dark hair flowing around her. She takes the last seat at our table, lays the menu, waves her hand over the top, it flies open and an entry glows a bright neon gold. All while she gives Bee the evil eye. The poor girl fidgets.

"Our turn, Bee." I expected some form of mind probe or sensation that something was filtering through my thoughts to see what I wanted, but nothing. The pages fly open and salad. I'm not too proud to admit my mouth is watering. I look over at Bee, eager to watch her get excited.

"Teriyaki tofu noodles with green beans. I..." She swallows. "I actually love that." The reverent wonder in her eyes slays me. Literally rips my heart from my chest and stuffs it full of compassion before ramming it back into a space that is now too small.

The food is thankfully quick to arrive. I lead the conversations and make our excuses the instant Bee and I are finished, swiping my card on the way out to cover everyone's meal. Back home, I let Bee choose a bedroom, say good night, and strip, barely getting shortie pjs on before collapsing on the bed and snoring. A sure sign I'm beyond exhausted.

Eighteen

Monday morning arrives with an achy back, sore limbs, and a massive headache. The giant tub with jets is tempting, but a shower will suffice. I have a houseguest to deal with.

I take my tea into the back garden to enjoy the peace and moderate morning temperature. Delicately scented flowers sway in the slight breeze, and I close everything from my mind except savoring a moment of tranquility.

When I can't delay any longer, I prepare breakfast and call Bee down. She shuffles downstairs, hair askew, eyes caked in sleep dust, and still holding a small, green, stuffed fish that was sitting on the bed. She yawns, stretches, and stares at the toy, shrugging as she puts it down.

I hold up options, and she chooses a healthy cereal and OJ. Making me feel very self-conscious for slathering thick strawberry jam on my doorstep toast.

"Are you vegan?" It's a logical place to start.

"No, I would be, but my harpy eagle needs some meat in our diet." There's a cold detachment in how she refers to her shifted side that I haven't heard with other shifters and does not seem healthy.

"That must get tricky, balancing the requirements of both of you. Your eagle is very large. I thought you were a dragon."

"I'm part ogre. I can transform as well as shift." She shrugs again, stuffing an overloaded spoonful into her mouth.

"Huh?" I stop myself from gawking at her and sip my apple juice. "How do ogres transform?"

Bee lifts her left hand, and it grows to twice its size but otherwise stays the same. Then it becomes much more robust, a hand I can imagine crushing skulls. I hide my shudder.

"Most ogres can change everything, getting big, like giants and stuff. I can't, just my hands and feet." Her eyes dart to me before scooting away. A second and third bowl of cereal goes as quickly.

"If you eat too much, you won't want lunch." I tease.

"There's lunch as well?" She bites back a curse, taking a deep breath.

"Bee, I don't know what your past was like, but, here, we have breakfast, lunch, and dinner. There are also snacks if you want them. Not that you have to stay here if you don't want to."

"Where else would I go?" The question flies from her lips before she can stop it.

"The GC would find you somewhere safe and comfortable. For the record, if you stay with me, there will be school, homework, and chores." I point the last of my toast in her direction.

"I can do that."

"How old are you?"

"Fourteen." She stammers. I cock my head sideways and raise an eyebrow. "Okay, I'm sixteen."

"Why lie? Another thing, no lies."

"Fourteen is old enough to be trusted with some independence and even get a job, but not old enough to be thrown out or sold off for money."

I choke, full on choke. Bee has to hit me on the back. Hard. After a coughing fit and a glass of water, I can finally tackle what she said.

"Which applied to you?" She's a pretty girl with a good figure, especially for her age, which probably gives me my answer, but I need to know for definite.

"Sold off. They were negotiating with several men about who would get me. I wanted to stay. Be a crusader, but it wasn't the plan for me." The life tumbles from her. Leaving an empty shell of the vengeful girl who snatched me up and promised me death, not that she fully meant it. Her voice drops to a sorrowful whimper. "I don't know if anything was signed."

"No one is forcing you to get married." Her mouth springs open with what I'm sure is an explanation that it doesn't need to involve marriage. I put my hand up to stop her. I am not naïve. I grasp exactly what she'd be used for but allow for some leeway with the language I choose to use. Plus, she's the one who set an age limit on it. "Or anything else."

"If the contract is signed, it cannot always be undone." She trembles, staring into the abyss of the future she imagines for herself. Fear gouges huge ridges into the bravado she's faking.

"If they come for you, they'll have to go through me." Which sounds tough and consequential but was nothing more than a gut reaction that I'm hoping I won't need to back up. I'd probably be alone, and, last time, had it not been for Draven, I would have fled.

My phone beeps a message from Sera, letting me know all newcomers to Whispering need to be announced prior to arrival or taken to the town hall as soon as possible. "We need to visit the town hall, and, please, no swearing in there."

"Be prepared for it to be anything inside." I warn Bee, preparing myself for today's crazy installment of what's behind the doors. I push it open, almost eager for another surprise cultural experience. I walk in and take in a... town hall.

Disappointment runs rampant until the tense, authoritative crackle in the air reaches me, and I snap to attention, searching for the recipient of my sudden urge to pledge allegiance. Bee huddles closer, peering around, not daring to move, even to breathe. While it is fraught, there's no sign of danger, and everyone is doing what they normally would, if with more purpose and a not-so-slight panic.

Lillie The All-knowing beckons us over, and I gladly head in her direction. "What's going on?"

"Jack is here." She gulps a mouthful of water and breath. "He's not happy."

My terror at hearing the EA eminence is on Whispering skyrockets at that. You remember me mentioning him? I had to turn the TV off and put a blanket over it when he announced essence people existed. Anyone who can invoke that level of nerve-destroying, soul-crushing reaction through a short, pre-recorded message on a TV screen is not someone to come face-to-face with.

"When is he leaving?" I'm already barrelling away, dragging a squeaking Bee behind me. My speedy progress towards the refuge of open space is halted by a solid wall. Big, strong hands wrap around my arms, steadying me, and I look way up into the face of the man I was trying to escape.

"I intend to be here for a few days." He gazes beyond my soul to every cloistered fragment of me, no matter where they sought refuge. Probably the same for my ancestors. Some of the studious severity slips from his expression with what I think is supposed to be cordial teasing. "I come in peace."

"Umm... good." He lets me go, and I take a step back, then another. There is no nickname for him. He is simply Jack The Eminence and every fiber of my being is compelled to wait for his command.

"Please, carry on with whatever you came here for. It's all business as usual." He bows slightly, and I tug Bee to the counter, keeping her out of his sight. Not that I believe he hasn't seen her. Nothing could escape those sharp eyes.

"He has that effect on everyone." Lillie guides us to a small table with a stack of forms in her hands. She gives about two-thirds to Bee. "You need to fill out these before you can leave."

Bee groans and takes them to another table loaded with pens.

"The top forms will get her assessed for aid and enrolled in school on the island." Lillie passes me several sheets of paper clipped together. "These are about her past. Do you need to talk in private?"

Before I can say no, we're surrounded by a hazy dome, and I'm leaning intently forward.

"No EA bigwig has been here before. Ever." Lillie's outward appearance is cool, calm, and collected, but her voice and one purple hair betrays her distress. "Anyone who leaves and joins the EA doesn't come back. Draven was the first."

"Never? No one?" My unease about my cutie notches up a level or two.

"Only for a short visit, but not to an official role." She stifles her rising agitation. "Now, Jack's here going through our records, interviewing the alphas. Something isn't right."

"Is it to do with The Adjustment?" Her face lights with understanding but fades to apprehension. "What do I need to do to make someone tell me what The Adjustment was?"

"You don't know?" She cries, jerking back and dropping her thin gold pen. She clutches her chest, taking short, sharp breaths. "Shit, Hector is coming. I've got to go. Fill these in, and she can stay with you."

Lillie leaves me with the forms and her pen. I complete them, doing my best not to be affected by her lingering anxiety, but it's so thick it's clogging my airway.

"I should go to the GC accommodation." Bee states over me, clinging the paperwork to her chest. I point to the other chair, and she sits.

"If that's what you want, I won't stop you, but you have a room." I quickly add, deciding not to let her think about it. If the type of person who would contractually purchase a child as if they are a commodity is potentially coming for her, she will not be secure enough there. "Have you met Jack before?"

"No. My family doesn't... couldn't afford to be near anyone in the EA." Her sad words hit me right in the feels. She perks up and grins. "What's for lunch?"

"I'm having a huge helping of sugar. Come on." I stuff my forms into my bag. I'll give them to Lillie when she can talk.

Over lunch, I find out Bee's family moved a lot to avoid the EA and Overseers. Her parents were killed pursuing their life of crime. Her brother left a few years ago, and she has no idea where he is or what he's doing. She can read but not good enough. I suspect it's the same for all her academic skills. There'll be a lot of hard work to catch up.

We leave the diner and take a slow stroll to Empy. Draven materializes from the bookstore looking holy edible in his warrior leathers, and strides forcefully in our direction. Raven appears right in front of us. It's a toss up what holds more menace, her weapons or the dark glint in her eyes.

"Are they going to hurt me?" Bee wraps her arms around her middle.

"No. But we need to ask you about your grandfather and his men." I reassure her as the distinct possibility she might not be as innocent as I've presumed sings songs through me. We make it to Empy, and I pause with the door handle half turned. "Before we go inside, I need you to be completely and utterly honest."

"You're scaring me." She takes a small step back, right into Draven, and springs forward.

"Good, because the Emporium does not mess around when it comes to keeping the artifacts in its charge safe. Do you have any intention now or in the future of illegally or immorally attempting to obtain anything you should not have?"

"Anything?" She squeaks.

"Anything." Raven drawls, polishing her sword with a yellow cloth. I roll my eyes at her.

Bee moves some loose stones with her foot, emotion swarms her face. Finally, her expression clears, and she raises her head boldly.

"I was told I should not have an education or a future beyond who they sold me to. So, yes, I will take what I am not meant to have."

"Beyond what should not have been denied you and a future not of someone else's choosing? Do you have any ill intentions towards the Emporium or anything within it?" Raven persists.

"No. I want a new future to claim away from crime and deceit." Her pride adds to the growing feelings I have for her.

"If you cannot answer a question, tell us." I push the door open and enter.

Nineteen

Empy greets me warmly, and I feel that extend to Draven and Raven but not Bee. She stands just inside, wide-eyed with goosebumps breaking out over her. The air around her visibly darkens and swirls as Empy probes her intentions with as much eerie drama as possible.

I cannot stop this or protect Bee. As much as I'm starting to have real affection for her, I am aware we have no solid proof she isn't up to something nefarious. I even have to concede she could be part of a larger plan to get a mole here, ready to stab us in the back. She may still be looking to avenge her grandfather. Not letting me die could be a ploy to gain my trust. But she does not have my trust, not fully. There is a tentative treaty that could build to more, but I do not trust easily.

Percy watches intently from his perch on the shelf. I moved him to the edge so he's not as isolated. After a bit, he returns to his default staring at nothing pose. I grab sodas, set them on the coffee table, and take my seat. I am about to tell Empy enough is enough when she stops, and Bee staggers to the sofa, pale and breathless.

Empy may have given her the okay to enter, but I can feel it came with a stark warning.

Raven takes the other chair, crossing one long leg over the other, her sword now back in its holster. We allow Bee to compose herself, although Draven is more intent with the space around her body, her aura. I wasn't going to look at it, but I cannot let go of any advantage I have.

Thick, gluttonous fear and trepidation are soothed by bright, tentative hope.

"I wasn't told much. Most of what I know is what I overheard, and I have no context." She says, running her finger around the rim of the soda can.

"Start wherever feels right." Draven growls. Empy is digging her claws further and further into him. Tunneling into his emotions and reactions and freely feeding them back to me. I filter most out because my cutie has strong opinions on a lot of things and is constantly weighing everything up.

"Things changed a few years ago," Bee says sadly, regret rolling around her like a chasm ready to engulf her. "Until then, my grandfather was in charge, and they got by with blackmail. People didn't get hurt, and it was sort of okay. Then it all changed. A man they called Mr. Sir promised them wealth, power, and prestige. He said the legendary book that had been changing the destiny of the world for many millennia was real, and he could get it. He convinced my grandfather to help him get it so they could make themselves immortal and revered by all. Rich and powerful beyond their wildest dreams."

I snag a glance at Draven and see the truth to Bee's words. My dream of the woman with my face furiously scribbling into a purple, leather-bound book hurls into my mind. I have no doubt they are one and the same.

My shock and Draven's unintended confirmation are not missed by Raven.

"Everything he said was a compliment, all of it. The sloppy, sickening type a man says to his wife when he's screwed up. From then, it got worse. I was treated like a possession, a servant. They stopped seeing me, I heard lots. They knew the man before and said constantly how much he'd changed. How much better he was. Everyone had sex with him and only him, but they were straight before. He had a hold over them they couldn't see, let alone break."

"Did any word or emotion come to mind when he was around?" Draven relaxes on the sofa beside her, doing his best to appear casual. Bee shakes her head, pushing further into the arm, away from him.

"I did think of them as his fangirls, ready to drop their pants with nothing more than a wink." She shudders with more than a faint sickly green pallor to her skin. "After years of searching and him screwing them stupid, they heard about an island that was born through the magic of the book to act as a protector of items of arcane magic. But nothing more, not its name or location until a few weeks ago."

"What changed?" Raven hasn't eased the intensity or venom from her glare.

"One day, they were sailing and saw the dome flickering. We couldn't get through, though. Three men died trying. Mr. Sir just told them how amazing they were and how sexy it would be if they swam, and they did. Not stopping until they..." Tears fall down her cheeks, her head falls back, and she struggles to talk. "One was my only friend. He gave me food. Taught me to read, he didn't even ask anything of me. He just swam around and around it with the boat following him and Mr. Sir calling how beautiful he was."

I reach over and rub Bee's arm as she sobs into a tissue. That's a lot of trauma packed into her young life. It's playing through her aura in a confused symphony of horrified terror. She'll need counseling, emotional healers, and time.

A necklace glimmers and glows in my peripheral vision. The long gold chain is made from decoratively interlocked links and oozes recovery and rejuvenation.

"How did they get through?" Raven's tone has finally lost its wrath.

"They timed it with the ferry. Mr. Sir located the store, and they planned the attack." Bee tells us in a rush, her body depleted of energy and overwrought with emotions. "He didn't die. He watched then fled."

"He's still out there?" Draven demands, and Bee flinches away, huddling in on herself, nodding.

"Thank you for telling us." I assert to ease Bee's fear and retake my chair. "What can you tell us about Mr. Sir? What did he look like, or what was his real name?"

She opens and closes her mouth, confused disbelief and possibly mental strain dominating her features. Eventually stammering. "I... I don't remember."

"Don't worry, I didn't expect you to. It'll be because of what gave him power over your grandfather and his men." Draven explains, for once, not scaring her rigid.

"Wear this. It'll help you feel better." I give her the necklace and more tears shine as she takes it from me.

"This is pretty, too pretty for me." She thrusts it back at me. "I can't."

I push her hands back, closing them around the decorative, precious, and charmed metal. "It's yours."

I lay a blanket over Bee as she sleeps curled into a tight ball on the sofa. She perked up once the necklace was on, but her exhaustion was starting to make everyone tired.

Draven stands and points outside.

"What do you know about the book?" Raven draws to her full, nearly six-foot height, her soot-black eyes sparking outrage. "You've been holding out on me."

I cannot voice anything about my dream. It's personal and private, almost sacred.

"I've heard rumors about a grimoire involving someone in the EA." It's Draven who breaks the silence. "They're all tight-lipped. I'll reach out and see what I can uncover."

"There's more," she grips his arm when he turns away, retrieving his phone.

"Loads, but I'm going to talk to Jack first."

"The eminence takes your calls?" Her eyebrows reach to her hairline.

"Don't be all 'the eminence takes your calls' like you two haven't been..." I nudge Draven as Jack steps into view. His mouth slams shut so tightly it couldn't be pried open with a crowbar.

The door glides open as Jack approaches, Empy encasing him in obeisance, almost to the point of being worshipful. Jack stands over Bee, and I'm propelled to her side, ready to defend. He waves his hand and turns.

"She cannot hear, even if she wakes." He folds into my chair, which expands to fit his huge frame. "The book was real and probably did all the things the legend said. It is now gone."

"Nothing with that much power simply goes away, Jack." Raven stands with her arms crossed, tapping her fingernails against her forearm. Jack regards her, his eyes racking over her body as she does his. Up close, this commanding man is one gruffly handsome bundle.

If he told me to jump, I wouldn't even ask how high because something deep inside me makes me accept him as a leader and protector. Even while another part of me sees the fractures in his control.

"The explosion. The gaping hole in the ground and destroyed buildings was no leaky gas pipe." Jack's grim, almost imperceivable nod not only affirms my statement but also that the Emporium was created through the magic of that book.

"But it's been changing destiny for millennia, it can't be gone." Raven marches to Jack, stands over him and scowls down. Barely contained waves of power cascade from him, forcing me to step back. "That kind of magic needs to be maintained."

"And yet it is gone." He drawls.

"What was in it?" Raven's voice has risen several octaves. "What are the consequences?"

"We wish we knew. Steps are being taken, but we are in the dark. Any light would be welcome. You are not to discuss this with anyone." His severe gaze cuts into me. "This information does not leave Empy or those closely affiliated with her."

With that, he's gone, with Raven right behind him.

"He's, umm... interesting." I sink into my seat, trying to make sense of what he said and what was left unsaid.

"Never a dull moment when Jack's around." Draven sneers, drawing my attention. He's engrossed with Jack and Raven's conversation, or rather, Raven speaking as if there was no tomorrow and Jack quirking an eyebrow at her.

"Those two have a thing going?" There was plenty of sexual tension between them but more the type that's of anticipation.

"There was something, some when. There are rumors she was his first."

"As in, took his cherry?" Draven nods. My heart skips a beat when Jack turns and glares at us. Both Draven and I scatter like school kids caught snooping and busy ourselves doing anything that doesn't involve us facing the window.

I dust a dust-free shelf with Jack's words ringing in my ears. I need to find out what the symbols from my dream mean. I find a pen and paper under the counter to write them on and focus on the memory, seeing her anguish, desperation, and fear. The urn she clutches tightly is bronze with inscriptions in the same language carved into it. Her tears fall onto the ground, soaking into the arid soil, giving it life and vitality. No matter how hard I try, I cannot put the symbols on the page. They stay just out of my perception until I put the pencil down, and they are clear. The instant I reach for it, they fade.

Raven marches back in, clenching and unclenching her fists. "That man is impossible."

"You didn't get anything more from him?" Draven asks over his shoulder.

She shakes her head. "I'm done here."

She's gone before I say goodbye or plead with her to stay. I'm honestly not above getting down on my knees. She's the only person who has an established link with Empy and can fight.

"She'll be back. I'm going to see if there are any signs of Mr. Sir around Whispering." Draven disappears, leaving me alone with a broken store, dangerous artifacts, and a sleeping teenager. Bluebell paws the door, and I let her in, bending to stroke her head. She meanders over to Bee, jumps up, and curls into her before snoring.

⚱️ ⚱️ ⚱️ ⚱️

Bee woke after an hour, saying she was hungry. A test to see my reaction, but her belly is now full.

"I have to check out the Learning Center." I say as we leave the diner.

Sal welcomes me with a crushing bear hug and vigorously shakes Bee's hand. He and the center are buzzing with positive energy.

"The timetable is expanding, look." His eagerness is contagious as he points to a large whiteboard now attached to the wall. "Sign up for something,"

I study the list, not sure what I can commit to.

"Can I?" Bee whispers, eyeing some course.

"Sure, you can." Sal offers a marker hanging from the wall on a long thin silver chain. She writes her name, carefully, reminding me of the twins when they started school. The letters sparkle and twinkle before disappearing. "It's magic. One of the witches spelled it for me."

"Wow, that's great." I lean over, trying to peer behind it.

"I can take the course? All twelve weeks?" Bee's astonishment has Sal reeling into an animated explanation of the Learning

Center and its purpose. To help as many people as possible gain the new skills or knowledge they require. Bee listens, transfixed. Her selection of basic letter and number skills for older teens and adults says too much. As the course is offered four times a week, I have to question the education on Whispering.

I wander further back, tuning into the building. Beyond the steady satisfaction of fulfilling a purpose and the motivation to inspire everyone within its walls is a yearning to do more. To grow and develop. It's all mirrored in Sal, his head is up, shoulders relaxed, voice bright, and smile warmer than the blazing in the bright sky sun.

Neither could be more different from how they were. A sense of achievement and pride flutters through my chest. Closely followed by blinding panic. If the book that created Whispering and everything it is truly is gone, what happens to Whispering?

Outside, people live their best lives, oblivious that their very existence is down to a woman scribbling symbols on a page.

The barren, desert-like wasteland from my dream is the antithesis of the utopia it has become. The dismal prospect of it all fading to the shadows of obscurity that nearly swallowed Sal stirs ice-cold shards of terror to trail through my veins.

A class on the notice board glows brightly as I approach it. The joy of ancient languages. An hour a week for six weeks, taught by Eragon, my Adonis. I sign up, recalling how his touch sent sparks through my body, and his breath fanned my neck, inviting me to tilt my head for his fangs.

SAMMI MASON

My hand rises to protect my neck as my name sparkles a dazzling blood red and disappears.

Twenty

I put the last of the groceries away. Shopping with a teen is a bizarre experience. They do not want to be there, but they also need to ensure you purchase everything. We had to borrow a trailer to tow behind the scooter.

Bee ended up signing up for several classes. Her stationery is sitting on the table, ready. At the moment, she's content in the garden munching on a bag of broken pretzels and a bowl of fruit with determined concentration etched onto her face as she works through a book Sal gave her.

"I'm going for a walk. You okay here?" Bee nods absently at me, her finger trailing across the page. I set off to soothe my restlessness and drive to explore the island. I follow the rocky cliffs past Empy and Store Row, to Main Town. The homes are less whimsical than Charmed Village but more colorful than those for the store holders. Most have large front porches with swinging chairs. Beyond that are rows of apartment blocks endowed with generous balconies. I watch as a woman steps from one, and blue wings extend from her back, allowing her to soar into the air. A few buildings over, a family arrives home in the same way.

Boats bob on the crystal clear water, some chug in and out of the harbor. If I venture further along the path, I'll come to Pack Village, home to most of the shifters. A lion and bat-eared fox trundle past me, and a horse gallops, heading in that direction. The lack of fear of wild animals is the most surreal part of life on Whispering.

The doors open in unison and the street is suddenly full of lively children tugging parents and older siblings towards the funfair. I follow, eager to see what's causing the excitement. The rides are silent and a man sits on a stage, book in hand. The kids sit cross-legged before him, all chatting and laughing. The instant he moves, they fall silent and have eyes only for him. He grows to twice his size and they cheer, chanting Titus.

He bows, falling over, and the entertainment begins. For the next hour, adults and children watch and listen, absorbed by his rendition of the story accompanied by funny voices, acting out scenes, and general merriment. At the end, he promises to be back next week and all the weeks. Many of the children head to the beach and splash around in the shallow tide as the temperature falls to friendlier levels. Not that anyone but me seems to notice the heat.

I see Gran walking along with Jerry and wave. In a mid-blue jumpsuit, strappy sandals, and her hair flowing around her shoulders, she's more chilled than I've ever seen her.

"Ah, Ginny, we were going for a drink." She links her arm through mine, not allowing me to say no. Or maybe I like the idea of her automatically including me. "There's a small bar around the corner that serves the nicest cocktails."

The bar is tiny, with only six tables and a display with more bottles than a supermarket. We snag the only empty seats, and, within moments, a gum-chewing, pink-haired young woman places three frou frou drinks in fancy glasses before us. "Magic?"

"What else? Try it." Gran sips hers and sighs. I try mine, and it's heavenly. Not too much alcohol, some cocktails knock your socks off.

"That is good." I drink some more, this time noticing it's a tad stronger than I thought. "You're very relaxed."

"Am I?" Gran looks down at her outfit and sweeps her hair behind her back. "I hear you have a houseguest."

"I do. She's a sweet kid." Gran's expectant expression does not encourage me to tell her more, and I'm not sure why.

"You'll have to bring her to the family dinner tomorrow." Gran pulls her phone out and starts clicking on the screen. "I'll do buffet style, it'll be less formal. Your great-grandfather can just put up with it."

"I have a great-grandfather? And other family?" She has never mentioned anyone apart from my father. Aunt Valeria wasn't revealed until I moved here.

"And you can finally meet them all."

"I'll look forward to it." She ignores the sarcasm that weighs down my voice.

"I'm going for a run." Jerry tenderly caresses Gran's cheek and nods to me as he shifts into a tiger, who nudges Gran's hand. She lavishes the creature with affection.

"You're different today." It wasn't meant to be an accusation, but if the cap fits.

"My granddaughter is finally here. I no longer have to venture to The Faraway. The Emporium has a keeper. Today is a good day." The blasé way she says this - considering it involved my life falling apart, my aunt disappearing, seemingly without trace, and a living storage for magical horrors going unguarded - does not sit right with me.

"What family do I have?" Is perhaps the most pitiful question someone in their forties can ask. Grans twists her lips, causing my chest to constrict.

"Many are hard to define." She turns thoughtful. "We are a mixed essence family. Some of us have a normal human lifespan, maybe a little longer if we are lucky, but others have been alive for hundreds of years. A few go back even further."

"What exactly is in our lineage, and could the twins have any of it?" The sudden thought squirms to the front of my mind.

Gran makes an unladylike grunting sound, spiking my annoyance. "Ruby has nothing. She is ordinary. Owen is a wizard, with another essence possibly developing."

"What the hell, Gran!" A few patrons turn to check and Gran waves them away. "You should have told me."

"Owen had his reasons for not saying anything." My anger at Gran is doused by that bombshell. I believed with every fiber of my being my relationship with my son was close enough for him to tell me anything. I know his childhood was far from idyllic. He didn't have his father's love, not like Ruby did. But he had two parents who were not fighting a custody case. But if my own son could not tell me something so critically significant, my best was not good enough. I failed as a parent.

"I need to go." I flee, ignoring her calling after me and attempt to outrun the relentless echoes of my own inadequacies. When my lungs are burning and legs are too shaky to continue, I sink down between tall fir trees. Huddling into a ball to ward off the raw chill invading my soul from every direction.

If Ruby had kept it from me, I'd shake it off. She opens up to Lawrence, not me. But it wasn't her, it was Owen. My son, who I made sure knew he was loved and valued. I thought our bond was strong. I try to figure out where I went wrong, but the jumble of my thoughts only rotates on him watching Lawrence and Ruby. Nausea rolls through my stomach, curdling the cocktail in my gut.

I lean back against the tree, letting my tears fall, doing all I can to ignore the ominous, menacing darkness chafing my skin and the shadows that move despite there being no wind.

The foreboding evil creeps ever closer, and my scream dies, snatched from me by a stampede of torment racing through my veins. I scramble to my feet and sprint in what I hope is the direction I came from.

Solid, strong arms lock around me. I kick, punch, and struggle for freedom. Biting the hand that clasps over my mouth, stifling my scream of terror.

"Ow! Stop, it's me." I can't place the voice, and I up my assault. "Rhett, the sheriff. Stop, I can get you out of here."

I freeze and let him drag me toward the light. Literally. The interwoven canopy of the trees casts dense, callous shadows all around. We reach the edge of the trees, and Rhett lets me go. I wrap my arms tightly around my middle, hoping with all the energy I have left it will ward off my trembling. It doesn't, but the understanding and lack of judgment in Rhett's tender gaze does.

I knew he'd be a shorts man, and his khaki cargo shorts and matching polo shirt proves me right. It occurs to me this outfit isn't much different from his uniform, but something tells me he's never truly off duty. I tuck that thought away, not sure why it stirs alarm bells.

Rhett jumps on a three-wheeled motorbike, holding his hand for me to climb on behind him. I cling to him, letting the glow of his benevolent radiance slay the oppressive gloom hanging over me.

When he pulls over, I get off and take several deep, shuddering breaths.

"Want to tell me why you were in Obscurity Forest?" His authority snags the last of my acumen.

"No." Honesty is all I can give him, and I truly do not want to admit to not being a good enough mother.

"I asked for that." A slow grin softens the grim lines of his handsome face. "In the future, do not enter Obscurity Forest unless you have a vampire with you. Failing that, me."

"Why you?" I'm too spent to be snarky and too wrung out to argue.

"I know how to get through them." The ghost of a distant memory eclipses his demeanor.

"Okay." I look around, realizing I have no clue where I am or how to get back home. "Can you direct me to the Emporium?"

"Would you prefer a lift?" I nod and climb back behind him. This time, noticing the invitingly muscular planes of his body beneath my hands, which may have decided to splay out and explore his six-pack.

He drops me outside mine, and I mutter thanks and run inside, not letting him voice the questions whirling around his mind.

The evening passes in a blur of dinner with Bee and falling into bed. Sleep eludes me as I stare into space, desperately trying not to think about where I went wrong.

I wake to a screech from the Emporium, warning that people with sinister intentions are there. I jump out of bed, throw on whatever I reach first, check for my leather bracelet and the protection it represents.

I don't need to slow as I purposely stride through the back door, the secret gate, and into Empy. I pause before entering the main store and wave my hand over the door, allowing me to see through it. Three men are trying with brute force to break the door down, their weapons catching the moonlight. Their horrifically deformed faces twisted into sneering growls are almost my undoing. I tap my bracelet and free my chain, spikes out, keeping it securely in my grasp.

I push into the main store, and their attention flies to me, the shock further contorting their grotesque, animalised features. I twist my finger, unlocking the front door, and they charge, rabid saliva dripping from their gangrenous mouths.

"Halt!" I dig deep on all I am, all Empy has, and channel my inner genie to put so much into that one word, but it does nothing. The rat-faced man charges at me, his long knife aimed at my gut. I whip my chain around his arm, yanking it back, leaving vicious gashes. The grungy, maroon blood spurting from the wounds doesn't stop or even slow him. I dodge to avoid being impaled and gather my chain, aiming it to encase his entire body.

His friends, Pig-face and Cockroach, attack the shelves, stuffing what they can into their pockets and tossing the rest across the room. It all lands on new shelves I create with nothing more than a thought.

Rat-face struggles to be free. The spikes claw through his tattered clothing to his flesh. Yet, he shows no reaction. I lift my free hand, calling a rope from the storeroom, and command it to secure him, not stopping until he's hogtied on the floor.

Pig-face starts up the ladder. I send the rungs around in a never-ending loop. He's too stupid or possessed to realize and too set on reaching the top to stop, effectively trapping himself. His piercing, savage oinks ruthlessly gnaw away at the courage I had painstakingly clawed together.

Cockroach screeches and squalls. I lock Empy down quickly, concerned he's calling forward more hideously deformed, animal-faced, humanoid monsters. He picks up Percy, whose fury becomes an audible cacophony of shrill clangs.

"Put. Him. Down." The command I manage has grown expediently, and Cockroach turns to me, rolling his head in weird angles, threatening to crush Percy. Which might be how he's released, but that is not a risk I can take.

"Ginny!" Draven pounds on the door. It never occurred to me he'd be locked out. "Let me in."

I lift my hand to let him in, but his abrupt yell stops me. He jumps back and shifts, breathing fire all over the narrow street. Cockroach gives a blood-curdling roar, and Percy flies from his grasp. I catch the thimble and tuck it between in my cleavage; it feels like the safest and easiest-to-reach place I have at this moment.

My chain flies from me, wrapping around Cockroach's neck. Bile rises in my throat as I yank it back with enough force to match the unadulterated violence shimmering in his eyes. That only grows more intense as his head rolls across the ground, landing at my feet. I kick it away, screaming as his body flails towards me, the same unnatural concoction as rat-face's blood oozing in rhythmic waves from his severed neck.

I grant my chain permission to extend and bind him from neck to feet. I call forward more rope, twirling my hand until he's engulfed, and draw my chain back.

Draven's fire has stopped raining down, and I flick the door open when he approaches and lock it down when he's through.

"How are you doing that?" He throws at me before yanking Pig-face from the ladder. Wrenching his arm up his back and wrapping an arm around Pig-face's neck, his oinking wails escalate, eroding any sense of goodwill I had left.

Propelled by something beyond my understanding, I lay my hand on Pig-face's chest, drawing his memories, and searching beyond the catastrophic, depraved magic, then do the same with Cockroach and Rat-face.

"Their humanity is gone. Their memories are nightmares. Their place in society, destroyed. They have lost the ability to shift. Their animal side has been erased. They have nothing left of the person they were or their humanity. They all need to die. It is the kindest thing we can do." I tell Draven with cold detachment.

He snaps Pig-face's and Rat-face's necks. He lifts Cockroache's now still body and grimaces. My stomach churns violently, and it's all I can do not to vomit as Draven drags all three outside, shifts, and incinerates them. I swivel my hand around Empy, and the grungy blood stains vanish. When he walks back in, and his lack of clothing finally registers, he's wearing tight black boxer briefs and nothing else. My internal body temperature heats so far up the scale anyone would think I hadn't gotten laid in forever.

The depressing thought that it has been months and, worse, years since I actually enjoyed sex rounds off my horribly miserable day.

I fetch bottles of water and practically collapse into my chair. Draven's throat must get sore breathing fire, and I'm just out of breath, hot, and sweaty.

"What were they?" Draven snags a drink, downing it in one.

"Someone's twisted magical attempt to combine the strength of each animal with the intelligence of a person." I resist the temptation to lick the drop of water that spills down his chin when he gawks at me.

"They were people?" He shudders, almost gagging.

"Shifters mixed with a pig, rat, and cockroach. I couldn't tell what their shifted sides were, it was gone." I roll a fresh, cold bottle against my chest, and touch my bracelet to rid myself of the thick leather garments. "I got what I think were their first names."

"We'll need to call the sheriff in." Draven reaches for his phone and shakes his head. "I'll be back wearing clothes in a second."

My eyes track his every step, luxuriating in how his buttocks move and back ripples. I mouth "mum-zoned," but it lacks the cold-shower effect it once did.

Draven returns moments later, fully clad in black jeans, a pale green Henley, and his bracelet. I'll need to remind him he shouldn't take that off for anything. He tucks his phone away. "He's on his way."

"What does he know about Empy?" This feels like something I should already know, not only as it's basic information but, as the Merchant, it seems like intel that should be inherited.

"Just about all of it. The sheriff always has. Want coffee?" Draven goes to the kitchen and starts a pot. The rich aroma soon fills the air.

"We meet again," my hunk rests a lean hip against the door frame. "Someone really should formally introduce us. I'm Rhett."

He steps closer, his gaze sweeping every inch of me, making me hyper-aware of the skimpy shorts and vest top that must be Ruby's, that, for some ridiculous reason, I put on. As I'm wishing I was in a more modest dress, I am. Rhett stops dead, cocking his head sideways.

"No one told me you were more than a genie."

"No one knew," Draven states, passing me my tea. "Not sure she was until tonight."

"That cannot happen, simply developing abilities," I assure them as a deep sense of harmony falls over me, calming my shot-to-hell nerves and ragged breaths.

"Yeah, it can." Rhett accepts a coffee and settles into the other chair. "Either through the phenomenon or a defunct heritage essence emerging."

"Pretend I have no idea what you mean." I wrap my hands around my warm mug.

"The phenomenon is where people randomly develop an essence for no reason anyone can discover. Many don't even have an ancestor who was essence. And, yes, the EA is doing research, and it is terrible what those people go through." Draven supplies, his tone curiously harsh.

"I've heard about that. I never believed the EA was keeping secrets." I give Draven a sideways glance. "Too many of those poor people have suffered too much."

Draven grunts, staring into his coffee. I can't help but wonder if he dealt with some of that in his former EA role.

"I am a genie; can't we grant wishes? Maybe I just granted my own wishes." They send me dismal, pitying looks.

"Ginny, genies lost their ability to grant wishes thousands of years ago. No genie has been able to grant a wish since." Rhett explains carefully.

"They'd probably terminate any who could." Draven huffs, sobering when he then takes in my alarm. "Life for most genies wasn't good. They were forced to grant wishes then were terminated when those wishes risked the secret that essence people existed. Eventually, the EA was forced to act, and that was when genies lost their powers. I only know this because I had a friend who was a doyen."

Harsh misery cascades through my body, woefully turning my inner swirling to a burdened confusion. I stare into my coffee, unable to process the last twenty seconds. Against everything else I've been through, done ,and found out, a decision that was made long ago should be insignificant, mean almost nothing, but it doesn't.

"I haven't heard about genies regaining their powers." Draven carries on as if he hasn't just turned my already skewed world on its head and kicked it into a spinning orbit for good measure.

"You have so much in your family line, it's hard to guess where the source of your magic is from." Rhett's reassurance melts into my turmoil.

"It's probably from the Emporium." I mutter because it sounds as good as anything else.

"That is possible." Draven is far from convinced.

"Empy has been known to loan a prospective Merchant abilities at times of extreme need." Rhett's thoughtful observation sweeps the Emporium before landing on me.

"That must be it." I crack open my connection to Empy, but all I get is the multi-voiced desperate howling of the artifacts trying to tell me their stories. I attempt to shove past that and find Empy, but she's been pushed even further back. Casting serious doubts on that theory.

"Anyway, it's not why I'm here tonight." My gaze instinctively strays to bloodstains on the dark wood floor. It may be gone, but I'll always see the congealed red goo.

"The Emporium was invaded by three men who were victims of magic meant to combine their intelligence with an animal's strength. It did not go well, and the men are dead." My bleak lack of emotion pokes at my conscience as their grossly animalized faces rattle around my mind. I write down their names and the animals they were mixed with and pass them to Rhett. He reads it, scrubbing his hand through his hair and down his face, expelling a long, unhappy breath.

"I think I know who each of these are. Two are loners, and the other often sneaks out to go drinking. They were easy targets." He tucks the paper into a pocket.

"There were four more, all cockroaches who didn't make it inside." Draven adds.

"What can you tell me about the magic?" Rhett opens a small notebook and starts writing.

"I don't know what there is to know." I rack my sore brain for anything else I can say about it.

"Ginny touched them and said, *their humanity is gone. Their memories are nightmares. Their place in society, destroyed. They have lost the ability to shift. Their animal side has been erased. They have nothing left of the person they were or their humanity. They all need to die. It is the kindest thing we can do.*" Draven says in parrot fashion. "Rhett, we don't have the same connection to the Emporium that Valeria did. And Ginny believed she was non-essence until a few days ago. We're learning as we go."

"I see." Rhett's brooding, emerald-green eyes burrow into me.

"Empy and I are growing in understanding and trust." I state, staking my claim on this peculiar place because, apparently, the last week hasn't been enough to scare me away.

"Right." Rhett drains his mug and stands. "If more comes to you, call me. I'll see what I can find out and report back anything interesting."

"It won't be dark for long. Let's get some sleep." Draven helps me to my feet and pulls me against him, shielding me from the horrors. "You did good."

Twenty-One

Tuesday, or at least the daylight hours, arrives with hideous music vibrating through the house, accompanied by a high-pitched squeal of someone who loves to sing. I roll over and bury my head under a pillow. It does nothing to block the racket.

I crawl from my comfy, warm bed into a scorching shower and limp downstairs. After battling bad guys without sustaining an injury, I twisted my knee while getting changed. As far as I'm concerned, it still counts as a battle wound and not merely a sign I'm falling apart at the seams.

"Morning." Bee yells as I turn the stereo down.

"Good morning." I snag painkillers from the cupboard, swallowing them with a glass of water and a tea chaser. Apparently, the hot liquid helps them dissolve and flow around the body more efficiently. But don't quote me. I have no idea where I heard that and no interest in finding out if the effect is psychosomatic.

"My Nexus profile has updated. I can enroll in school and get a job." Bee plonks down opposite me at the kitchen table, thrusting a plate of eggs and toast in front of me.

"Thanks." I'm not used to someone cooking for me, especially breakfast. She shrugs it off like it's nothing. "Where is the school?"

"Main Town." She pokes her eggs around her plate, peering at me through the tops of her eyes.

"Is there any set time for us to be there?" She shakes her head. "I need to check in on Delly at the store. We can go straight after."

Bee nods, and her mouth, like her face, slams shut. It's as though she's suddenly taken a vow of silence. Part of me wants to leave it, to let her talk in her own time and not push, but I don't know her well enough to know if she will. She could keep whatever is going through her mind clammed up tighter than a duck's behind forever.

"Bee, if you have something to say or ask me, go for it."

She sags in her seat, cramming her mouth full of eggs and making a show of struggling to eat it. I can't help but chuckle.

"Why?" springs from her, followed by alarm.

"Why what?"

"Why are you helping me?" Her voice is so small and threadbare, it's pitiful.

"There are loads of reasons. You deserve better than what you had." I'm certain I've said that before and convinced I'll be saying it again. "I want to make sure you stay on the right path and don't stray into trouble. You need to be kept safe, away from anyone involved in your past."

"But I tried to ki..."

"You pulled me from the ocean and saved my life." I butt in. Yes, she was the person to drop me in it, literally. "It's not like you're going to need to pull me out again, is it?"

"No, no way, never ever. I promise." She frantically shakes her head.

"I'll check in with Delly, and we'll head to the school." I give her a comforting smile as I settle in to eat with her before we leave together to check the store and head to school.

I hear Delly panting before the door of the Emporium is even open. She's on her hands and knees, furiously scrubbing the floor, her arms moving with a frenzy that has to be killing her back. Her top is soaked with sweat, her hair falling from the bun she tied it in, wisps sticking to her face. The acrid scent of chemicals hits me as I march closer to stop her tirade, and my worry for her surges higher.

"It doesn't feel clean. I can't make it feel clean." She whimpers. I crouch over her and lift her hands, silently asking Bee to fetch a towel from the kitchen and guide Delly to the sofa.

"I'll be at the Learning Center." Bee says quietly, wincing as she passes me the towel.

"There was an incident last night, and the floor got dirty," I tell Delly softly, taking in the tense strain around her eyes and downward turn to her mouth as I dry her hands. "How long have you been cleaning for?"

"Dunno." She stares at the bucket. "Maybe if I add more bleach."

"More bleach? Delly, have you been putting your hands in bleach?" She says nothing. I lift the towel, horrified at the bright red patches and take a good sniff. It reeks of a mix of strong cleaning chemicals. "Let's rinse it off your skin before it does any lasting damage."

I drag her into the kitchen, where far too many bottles lay empty around the sink. The water turns red and brings tears to her eyes, but her tormented gaze remains steadfastly on the floor.

"I think we'll leave something down that will make it clean, so we need to stay outside today. Is that okay?" Her bottom lip quivers. "I can't see the mark. I'm surprised you can."

"Shifters have good sight and smell." Delly tells me. Her voice drops to a whisper. "Empy stinks of death, and she doesn't like it."

"Is it her or you that's making you scrub the floor?" Delly purses her lips and turns her back on me as she carefully pats her hands dry. I twist her to face me and rotate her hands to see her palms clearly and battle to stay calm when I glimpse how torn up they are. She must be in agony. "Honey, you can't let yourself get hurt like this."

"But Empy doesn't like it." She insists, shuffling her feet.

"But she's okay with your hands being ripped to shreds, blistered and bleeding?"

"Shhh." Delly spins around as a blast of enraged air swarms her. At least I can release the worry that Empy is harming Delly, but I will have to lay down some stringent rules.

"We appreciate your dedication, but neither Empy nor myself want you to be in pain, especially when it is avoidable."

"But Empy doesn't like it." The anguish etched into Delly's features tells me this runs much deeper.

"Well, Empy can use her magic to sort it out then." I mean this to be gentle, but it isn't. Delly bites her lip, almost to the point of breaking the skin. "We'll talk some more later. Let's get your hands sorted."

"But Empy doesn't like it." Delly stamps her foot, and I resist the urge to chastise her like a child.

"Empy, please, demonstrate to Delly how much more you dislike the damage to her hands than you do the state of your floor?" I call out, and a gust of wind catches Delly and physically lifts her outside. I follow, grabbing our bags as I exit. "Delly, has that shown you anything?"

She nods and wipes her eyes.

"The Emporium and I care about you and your welfare. Please, don't give either of us a reason to decide you cannot be there alone." I suspect my limits are lower than the Emporium's. To be honest, I'm nearly there at the moment. Seeing sweet Delly like this is disturbing on so many levels. "Where is the medical center or doctor?"

She points to the end store on the other side of the row, and I walk her over. Explaining what happened is easier than I expected, but I suppose everyone on Whispering is used to how the stores function. The treatment is also a lot quicker. She's given an elixir that heals her hands within minutes of drinking it. They give me one for Empy, and I spray it, convincing Delly to go home and rest while it soaks in and does its thing.

She shuffles unhappily up the street, vowing to be back tomorrow. When she reaches the corner, she turns around, sees me, and her shoulders sag. Plastering on a fake smile, she slowly ambles away. Delly's devotion is rapidly sliding from admirable to alarming.

I enter the Learning Center and get a waft of the sense of purpose that's mirrored in Sal's eyes, despite how tight his brow is drawn as he listens to Bee. He sends her to pick a book and strides in my direction.

"Is Delly okay?"

"She's fine after treatment. I've sent her home." I'd love to know how much Sal knows about the Emporium, especially as he's one of the few who will tell me without talking in riddles or waiting for me to discover it myself. "I'm going to get Bee settled into school, then I'll pop back. Will you be busy?"

"No, I'm only the supervisor today." With that, a crowd of people leaves, all waving and thanking him, and another group walks in and heads down the stairs to one of the new lower levels. "But I do need to help them set up."

Twenty-Two

Signing Bee up for school took less time and effort than it should. There were no questions about her family or situation, not even her current academic attainment. They simply assigned her a locker, handed her the relevant books, and off she went to her first class. I like things to be straightforward. Who doesn't? But imagine that scenario anywhere else in the US. The UK would be no better.

We weren't even asked for a birth certificate, which is just as well because we don't have it, and Bee has no idea how to get one.

My trip to the Town Hall to talk to Lillie was unhelpful. She was run off her feet, and her hair was a dark, dull purple. She didn't so much as look at me when I handed over Bee's paperwork. Sal was just as busy when I popped my head into the Learning Center. He was perched against the edge of the counter, deep in conversation with another man about the benefits of teaching a wood turning class.

Ready to rest my knee, I do my best not to limp back to the Emporium.

"What happened?" Draven asks as I open the door and find him drying the floor.

"Delly scrubbed it with enough cleaning products to fill a small country until her hands were bleeding." I clench mine to stop them from trembling. "Draven, why didn't she stop, or why didn't the Emporium tell her enough was enough?"

He blows out a long breath. "The Emporium should have. Would have in the past. Before you ask, I have no idea what that means beyond the obvious."

"Did you know some of the artifacts tell her to do not good stuff? She didn't elaborate." I sink into my chair and rest my foot on the coffee table to elevate my knee.

"I'll get her to show me which ones, they may need to be concealed from her." His gaze sweeps the room, and he huffs.

"Like my genie lamp?" Its allure still reaches out to me, caressing my consciousness.

"Let's hope not." Draven's stare hardens.

"Also, why was it so easy to enroll Bee into school?" Not wanting him to dwell on my lamp, more questions fall from my mouth. "And why do so many people here need help with basic education skills? How were you able to dispose of the bodies without anyone questioning it or investigating?"

"That's a lot of questions." He sighs, walks into the kitchen, and clicks the coffee machine on.

"Can I have a soda? I have more, many, many more." I call. They're tumbling from me in a great cascade.

"Yeah, I have a few as well." He passes me my drink and sits on the sofa with his mug. "Before the Academy, I saw the island differently. Then, visits were a vacation, almost a trip to an alternative reality. It all felt ordinary, peaceful, as if this was how the whole world should be but couldn't."

"And now?" I watch his chest rise and fall with a deep sigh.

"I've fallen back into old habits that took me years to break. Accepting things as normal despite them being bizarre and fundamentally wrong, perhaps immoral, and possibly against everything the EA stands for." He sits forward, resting his elbows on his knees. Gazing at the steam floating from his strong brew. "All my EA experience is screaming at me that nothing here is as it should be."

"Should I bother to ask how it should be?" His brow and shoulders lift then drop in the universal 'beats me' motion.

"Life used to be straightforward, and my path across it mapped out. Now it's a maze that may not have a center to find." Bitterness stews in those words, ready to fester.

"Did you discover anything more about the book?" There's no pretending we don't know what book I'm talking about.

"Not yet, but I've put feelers out, which might come with more visits with more EA officials, but their input could be... interesting." He deliberated long and hard over that last word, giving me, guess what, friends? Yep, more questions.

"That may not go down well." And I am not inwardly grinning at the prospect of poor old Oompa greeting a barrage of EA alphas, betas, and whatever else they have. "Could we get Jack to open up more?"

"Have at it and see." Draven's eyes soften, and his mouth curls slightly upwards.

"What's a good way to get him talking?"

"Make him angry, then he'll ball you out for hours."

"No. I don't fancy that idea." I shudder, wishing and hoping I never experience that. Bluebell jumps up on my lap, turns around to get comfy, and nudges my hand for attention. "Can you tell us, Bluebell? I bet you've seen more than most people."

"She's been the same since I was a kid." Draven says, thoughtfully regarding the scruffy, ginger feline. Bluebell cracks an eye open and meows.

I guess him to be late twenties, possibly a bit older. Cats can live as old as thirty, although it's rare, but when Draven says she was the same, I anticipate he means exactly the same. I lift her up, with her front legs dangling, and study her grumpy face. Intelligence, indigence, and I'm pretty sure she's telling me to sod off.

"Could she be a shifter?" She rolls her eyes at me.

"Never known anyone shift into a domesticated cat." Draven shakes his head.

"Not a shifter, but you are not a normal cat, are you?" Her meow is the most catlike sound you could hear.

"Although this is Whispering, Bluebell could be unique." Bluebell sends Draven the dirtiest look I have ever seen, and Rose's are famously epic. Some days, it feels like two-thirds of the GIFs are her 'die-painfully' stare. He holds his hands up, "I stand corrected. Bluebell is definitely unique."

"You're an untapped treasure trove of information, aren't you, sweetie?" I croon at her. Bluebell hangs from my hands, glaring at me.

"You both got a minute?" Rhett asks, striding in strain and exhaustions drawing his face in to tight lines that look out of place. He goes straight to the kitchen, pours them both a coffee, and practically collapses into the other chair. Sera follows and perches uneasily on the edge of the sofa. Her usually pristine blouse is rumpled and stained, a cacophony of the unspoken twisting her face.

"You look absolutely beat," Draven says, taking in Rhett's five o'clock shadow, crumpled clothes, and the fact he's laid back, ready to nod off.

"It's been a morning. There are more unaccounted-for shifters. It's like they vanished into thin air." Rhett sips his coffee as if his life depended on it.

"Do you have sniffer dogs?" I butt in helpfully. Rhett and Draven exchange a pained look and turn to me, their brows drawn sympathetically. "You don't need sniffer dogs. You are shifters."

"Atta girl." There's a touch more disdain in Draven's voice than I appreciate. Rhett's lips purse as he gives Draven the side-eye. Sera's mouth hangs a tad open.

"I have all the deputies searching, but no one is hopeful of finding them. As people anyway."

"All of the deputies?" Draven sits forward sharply.

"All I could round up." Rhett runs his hand through his hair.

"The coven has also scoured the island." Sera taps her foot nervously. "We've never had to do that before. The High Priestess asked me to stress that. Forcefully. No fae or wizard found anything, either, it wasn't just us."

"Sera, no one doubts the coven's efforts or abilities. If this was a usual situation, I wouldn't need to call them in." Rhett assures her. "I'm grateful they tried."

"What was found?" Draven prompts. Rhett grimaces. "Someone must have found something."

"Nothing." Rhett scrunches his face at this as though that admission left a foul taste in his mouth.

"Nothing? As in nothing, as in not anything at all?" Draven's disbelief acts like reading something in a larger, underlined, and bold font with exclamation marks. My heart sinks to my feet, weighing my legs down.

"That's the nothing," Rhett confirms. His bleak dread sends shivers down my spine. He turns to me with far too much foreboding. "A quick lesson about life on Whispering. I'm the police, just me. Unless something happens, and I need to bring others in, then I have a huge chunk of the island at my disposal. They range from shifters, wizards, witches, and fae, and whoever the hell else I can get my hands on. If I call everyone, it's big and bad and time to worry. The last time a sheriff called in more than two people was about four hundred years ago. When Raven decided not to play nice."

"Ohh." I gulp the lump in my throat. Friends, which bit of that do I digest first? The snippet about him needing to call a huge chunk of the island? And they still found nothing? There possibly being more hideously deformed animal-people? That Raven doesn't always play nicely? What the hell does not play nicely actually mean? Or maybe why I feel I should share my visions about the book with Rhett, but not Draven?

We don't say anything for a long while. And those questions are added to the ones I already had going through my head like a broken record or a horribly repetitive song.

"Raven was after something from the library, not the Emporium. It wasn't a Merchant thing." Sera adds as an afterthought.

"I gotta go. I have a meeting with Jack." Rhett salutes us goodbye as he leaves.

"What?" I ask Draven as shards of an unvoiced warning shimmer over his aura.

"It is impossible for them to find nothing." He mutters, leaving me searching for a needle in a haystack that means something here isn't completely busted.

"I promise you we tried." Sera insists.

"We don't doubt that," Draven responds, his dragon making a stark but brief appearance in his eyes, no less perplexed than the rest of us. "But Whispering just doesn't work like that. We both know the sheriff should be able to locate anyone from the Island anywhere in the world or anyone on the island, no matter where they are from."

"Yet, somehow, he can't find any trace of them, at all." I supply. "Does it all come back to the book?"

Sera's gaze darts to me with her own questions.

"Or The Adjustment, which is related to the book." Draven rubs his forehead. "If it is all connected..."

"Don't say it." I plead with him because not saying something makes it not true, right? Sadly wrong.

"The facts as we understand them." He blows out a long breath, and I twist my mouth because his facts might differ from mine. "The Emporium is the genuine purpose of Whispering, which likely has some relation to the book. Which is now gone forever. The demise of the book caused The Adjustment, which led to Valeria leaving." He stops talking and sighs mournfully when his niece and nephew walk past with a couple. The resemblance between man and boy can only be father and son.

"Is someone ever going to tell me about this book?" Sera's stricken whisper is bursting with the emotions I'm trying to contain. I nod at her, wishing there was a way to wrap it in a bow.

"What will all that mean?" I curse my lack of understanding of not only the Emporium and Whispering but all things essence.

"Well, it could, at least in theory, contaminate the magic of Whispering." Draven's words contain something that doesn't sit quite right, but I can't put my finger on it.

"How much of the island is based on magic?" I rub my chest to ease the constrictions squeezing my lungs.

"All of it." Sera's healthy, tanned complexion has gone ashen as her chest is rising and falling rapidly.

"Every damn thing on the island, from the stores to the people, are all somehow completely and irreversibly dependent on that magic." He gives the answer I knew was coming and didn't want. He walks to the window and stares out.

"Could one of the witches or wizards fix it?"

Draven takes my suggestion more seriously than I thought he would but shakes his head after a few moments. "It isn't their type of magic."

"Does that matter?" Empy's tense fear wraps around me, not hiding her fierce determination to protect everything within her walls from those who seek to exploit their powers and everything outside of them from some of the evil, reassuring me that she shields. It's another somber reminder of why the balance on Whispering cannot fail.

"Yeah, different types of magic, whether witch, wizard, or fae, and the rest all work in different ways. They don't exist together, and even if they did, they wouldn't mix well enough to work." Draven doesn't see Sera stiffen with blinding panic, and he obviously doesn't know she is all those things.

"Could a fae, witch, and wizard work together to make the magic?" I ask, not prepared to reveal Sera's secret.

"They wouldn't know where to start, no one has found magic like Whispering's. It is exclusive to the island. Any attempt to alter it could destroy it instantly."

"Then we have to find something."

"What?" Draven turns on me, standing over me with his arms fiercely crossed over his chest, anguish for those he loves scorched through every atom of his being.

"That I do not know, but it starts here, with the Emporium." I declare, scanning every inch, all the nooks and crannies, for an answer. A clue will do. At this point, I'll take anything.

Guided by an invisible force, I stand tall behind the counter as emotions and sentiments crash over me as a universe of legacy knowledge smashes into my head. Overwhelming my mind with a million and one voices, all wretchedly wailing to have their stories heard. In there somewhere is the subdued, frenzied whisper of the Emporium desperate to be heard.

I pledge a vow to find and reclaim Empy so she can rise to her former glory. Sealing my fate as the Merchant, a merciless role that requires life and death judgments to be made in a millisecond, with both complete compassion and utter ruthlessness. An icy chill shoots down my spine, as the consequences of getting this wrong hang heavy on my shoulders.

My most loyal companions are a reluctant dragon shifter with his own agenda, and a seamstress witch who possesses the types of magic that are dangerous to mix. A flamboyant vampire with a flair for stating the negative and a ragtag group I've only known for a few days. I already adore them, it would be crushing if they were not all they seem.

Best not to forget the possibly not a cat cat. That creature has an extraordinary story to tell, if only I could find a way to hear it.

And not only must we guard dangerous magical artifacts from unprecedented evil, but we also need to preserve the way of life of the people who call Whispering home. Even though none of it should exist.

My midlife adventure has gone from enthralling to a lethal challenge that may still prove beyond my limits, but I don't have the luxury of failure. Too many people are depending on me, and the eerie sting of incoming peril floats around us in a blood-curdling foreboding.

Can Ginny juggle battling sinister forces, while keeping Paige and the bookshop in solid forms, all without losing her genie cool? **Continue the adventure in *A Genie's Perilous Predicament!***

Meet Sera, and explore Whispering before the Adjustment ripped it to shreds, in The Emporium's Mercenary Merchant. And claim your copy of Tara, to discover this amazing world before the secret of essence people was exposed.

Reviews are like treasure maps leading fellow readers to hidden gems and gifting authors with heartwarming treasures.

A Note From Sammi

I live on the south coast of England with my two almost grown-up children. They have both inspired characters, but for the sake of a peaceful like, I'm not about to reveal which. When I'm not writing, I love finding a moment to enjoy a great book and a mug of steaming tea.

I adore creating magical tales set in enchanting locations with strong, witty heroines and swoon-worthy heroes.

My Newsletter is the best way to get updates on my writing, ensure you don't miss any releases or special offers, and find out about my chaotic life.

You'll also receive Tara, and The Emporium's Mercenary Merchant, two short stories.

Find all the best ways to follow me.

Reviews are like treasure maps, leading fellow readers to hidden gems and gifting authors with heartwarming treasures.
A few words or a rating would be amazing.

Printed in Great Britain
by Amazon